TACENDA LITERARY MAGAZINE

Edited By
SHIRIN KARIMI

Cover design
LIZ CALKA

Text Design
EMMA LYDON
SABA TABRIZ
REBECCA WEISENHOFF

Associate Editors
CARLA MAVADDAT
CHRIS MILLER
SABA TABRIZ

BleakHouse Publishing

2011

First Printing: April 2011

ISBN: 978-0-9797065-8-5

Printed in the United States of America

EDITOR'S NOTE

The short stories, poems, and photographs featured in the Spring 2011 edition of *Tacenda Literary Magazine* contribute another layer to our understanding of the multifaceted world of crime and punishment. By offering unique and contemplative insights into the justice system, the works featured here both educate and illuminate the public on the dark corners of our society that we ignore at our peril.

We are afforded many glimpses into this hidden world with the variety of pieces included here. Works like Emily Heltzel's "Until Next Time" and Gretchen Cruz's "Lights Out" offer our audience a sense of empathy for prisoners whom we will never meet. In their poignant short stories, we are finally able to remove the brand of "Prisoner" from the characters and witness how powerful human emotions can emerge and find expression behind the prison bars. In another look at prison, Tim Gallivan, Kerry Myers, and Charles Huckelbury expand on the terrifying, lurking danger on their eloquent commentaries on Robert Johnson's novel, *Miller's Revenge*. Similarly, "Empty Cell Windows," dramatist Ellen Kaplan's stage adaptation of the original story by Sonia Tabriz, and the short story, "Ariadne" by Hannah Herbert, allow for a different perspective on the cell, the most suffocating enclosure of the human spirit.

The poetry included here such as Zachary W. Faden's "The Day That Never Ends", Allison Whittenburg's "Words Leave Me Hungry", and Franziska Kabelitz's "Integration" provide a beautiful voice to thoughts never spoken aloud. Their themes of aborted dreams and desperation reveal the sadness following a lost future, terminated human potential, and the desire for something more than the prison, or home, can offer.

And finally, works like Rachel C. Cupelo's *Bullied* exposes a heartbreaking and all-too-familiar look at the tragedy that results from injustice. Just as we at *Tacenda* reflect on each submission in a blind-review process, the works in this edition force us to remove the lens of judgment and bias through which we see the world and see our society with perfect clarity. Perhaps with this new perspective and the inspiration drawn from art, we can endeavor to create waves of righteousness in the ocean of wrongs.

Shirin Karimi
Editor-In-Chief, *Tacenda Literary Magazine*

TABLE OF CONTENTS

STORIES, POEMS, PLAYS

"Until Next Time"
Love Letters from the Inside

By Emily Heltzel

Sarah Hendrickson 7278176
Maryland Correctional Facility for Women
7943 Brockbridge Road
Jessup, Maryland

May 3, 2004

Dear Shane,

I've been here for six months, and yesterday was the first time I had a true conversation with my cell buddy, Julie. She asked me about how and when we first met, and I immediately saw your face reddening with embarrassment, just like it always did when people asked us this question. I just love telling the story, and I still remember it like it was yesterday, even though it seems like a lifetime away – first semester, freshman year at GW. I was out of my element in a general business course – why did I *ever* think that would be a good idea? I've always been too soft for the cutthroat business world. You sat across the aisle from me, and I had always thought you were cute in that nerdy sort of way. One day you angrily raised your hand to counter the "profit at any cost" mentality that our professor was advocating. You questioned the morality of such an approach, and then proposed an alternate model – one that generated profit without, in your words "further screwing the impoverished in the process." I was hooked. "Cute, smart and articulate, and – wait for it – *he cares about the poor!* I think I'm in love," I joked to my roommate that night. Those remain some of my favorite traits of yours.

I skipped my last two classes that fateful day that I finally worked up the courage to talk to you after class (with the smooth opening line "So… um… what did you think of that test?"). Grabbing coffee after class (to discuss the test, of course!) turned into lunch…which then turned into walking around the Mall at sunset. We never once ran out of topics to talk about, and I remember returning to my dorm room with a newly acquired understanding of the phrase "giddy as a school girl."

That feeling of utter happiness never faded after the first date. The thoughtful notes I would find tucked into my notebooks (*"Even though I haven't seen you yet, I know you look beautiful today"*) would seem forced and cheesy in any other situation – but they were from you, and they were perfect. You didn't just hear me – you truly listened to me. I trusted you beyond a doubt – a feeling I never had before knowing you. I was truly content for the first time in a long time. With you, I finally felt safe. It was at this point that I concluded the story for Julie- mostly because I could hear your embarrassed voice in my head telling me that I was starting to ramble. I can't help it, though, Shay – past the point of reason, I was, and am, a fool in love. Until next time…
Forever yours,
Sarah

Sarah Hendrickson 7278176
Maryland Correctional Facility for Women
7943 Brockbridge Road
Jessup, Maryland

November 3, 2004
Dear Shane,

Julie asks a lot of questions about you. At first, I found it a little strange – being in here has made me forget what genuine interest in anything other than your own concerns looks like. In any case, I'm grateful to her for inspiring me to write to you. When it gets particularly straining in here, I take refuge in our love, because as much as I enjoyed falling in love with you, nothing could ever compare to *being* in love with you. I oftentimes had to remind myself in the beginning that you couldn't possibly be as perfect as you seemed. And in some ways, you weren't: your awful sense of direction resulted in hours (and tanks of gas) wasted, hopelessly lost. You never put my books in the right order on the bookshelf (alphabetical by author, then in chronological order according to the original publishing date – not that complicated!), and you preferred Guns N' Roses to Bruce Springsteen (seriously, who could prefer *anyone* to the Boss?). But you were passionate and thoughtful, caring and intelligent, and you loved me – and each day I found myself more in love with you.

I began to list for Julie the things I learned from our relationship, and the list rapidly grew to a considerable size. You taught me how to share – a lesson I should have been taught long ago, except that no one seemed able to find the time to teach me. With you I learned to share myself – the ultimate leap of faith, but one that I willingly took for you. You taught me that I was capable of trust, and then you spent every day proving that you were worthy of my trust. You taught me to not take everything so seriously, even eventually getting me to (begrudgingly) admit that the world would not end if my books were out of order on the bookshelf. Although throughout the course of our relationship I have come to find that you are indeed human (and thus imperfect), I love every single one of your imperfections. Together, we embraced life with an appreciation of everyday miracles – such as the sunrise over our favorite city – and took life's challenges in stride. We were the definition of a dynamic duo and I never grew tired of being a part of what our friends referred to as the "it" couple. Until next time…

Forever yours,
Sarah

Sarah Hendrickson 7278176
Maryland Correctional Facility for Women
7943 Brockbridge Road
Jessup, Maryland

May 3, 2005

Dear Shane,

Remember when we were in college, and I would reward myself with showers? "Five more pages of this paper and you can take a hot, relaxing, half hour shower!" I would tell myself. Of course, around page two I would give in and you would tease me that I could never stick to a schedule — but I never had to, because you would always make sure we were on time. I'm not sure you would recognize me if you saw me now. I am told when to dress and undress, when I can shower, when I can eat. My life is completely at the mercy of the merciless guards; although some nights we'll get lucky and Baghley will be the main CO. Sometimes, if you're feeling generous, it's not altogether impossible to convince yourself that Baghley has a soul — something I just can't seem to believe with any of the other COs. While the other COs make it a point to come to my cell first after dinner has been served (and then punish me for insubordination when my food is not eaten), Baghley will collect my food tray last, because he — like you — has come to accept how slowly I eat. It may not seem like a lot, but here it's everything.

One thing I've learned is that life stops on the inside. The sooner you acknowledge this, the better chance you have of maintaining some semblance of sanity. It's heartbreaking the day you realize that the lives in which you once played such an integral role are continuing and thriving without you. Jamie O'Reilly came to visit not too long ago. You remember her, right? She was my first real friend in DC; we used to be inseparable. I'm not sure she'll be back — it was just so hard for the both of us. It took her about a half hour to tell me a simple story because I had to keep asking for clarification. I didn't even know she had a second child — she began a story about her son Jacob, and I was immediately at a loss — the last I had seen her, she was pregnant with little Elisa. Elisa is almost three now — walking and talking up a storm. Our friends always said we would be the first to have children. Can you imagine Jamie as a mother of two? Where does the time go??

My life on the outside is not my life here; the person I am here is not who I was then. My lengthy internal conflicts about whether I could get away with wearing my favorite black boots with my brown dress used to be my biggest concern on a Friday. Sorry for subjecting you to all of those painfully and unnecessarily difficult decisions. Now I worry that they will confiscate my Spanish book (acquired after 4 long months of waiting) before I master the present tense. My self–imposed "shower rewards" are long gone now, too; everything I do is predetermined for me. Those choices that meant nothing to me are no longer mine to make. They were mindless, maybe, but they were meaningful because they were mine… meaningful choices because my life was mine to live. Only now that I'm confined in this hell can I finally find the value in something so obviously priceless. Life stops on the inside.

Until next time…
Forever yours,
Sarah

Sarah Hendrickson 7278176
Maryland Correctional Facility for Women
7943 Brockbridge Road
Jessup, Maryland

November 3, 2005

Dear Shane,

I think this place is starting to get to me. Julie has said that she's worried that I'm withdrawing, but I'm not even sure if that's possible – because honestly, what is there to withdraw from? This life isn't a life. I don't want you to see me like this. I don't want our friends to see me like this. I don't want my family to see me like this – weakened, exposed, and vulnerable to the whims of the corrections officers. My quality of life is largely dependent on their perceived quality of life – disputes with wives or girlfriends, disputes with bosses, bad commutes to work: these are just a few of the many factors that can have a huge effect on our treatment for the day. I'm sorry that their life of freedom is so difficult. Going home and sleeping in a fluffy queen-sized bed must be really frustrating. Being able to choose when and where to eat, when to sleep, where to go – why can't they see how lucky they are?! They see us every day – trapped in cages; not dead, but not really living – and they can't be grateful for the lives they still have? It's revolting.

I know there are people that think this desire is hypocritical and without basis – that the fact that I have *nowhere* to turn – physically or emotionally – is of my own doing; this is, after all, prison. But there's nothing unreasonable about the desire to matter… the desire to, at the very least, hear and be heard. Those in power know that this desire is at the very essence of humanity, and so they take it away as punishment for wrongdoing – the very cruelest of cruels. Hope and humanity are privileges that don't exist here.

I'm sorry that this letter has been so bitter. I never mean to take out my frustrations on you, but somehow it seems to happen, doesn't it? I guess that was always one of the flaws with our relationship: I've always been so comfortable with you that nothing was off-limits: every little annoyance and frustration was aired out and vented thoroughly, in whatever way I deemed appropriate. Sometimes I find myself awestruck at my old behavior: the unfounded fears, the irrational notions – you knew my past and what I've been through, so maybe that helped, but I still sometimes wonder how you put up with me during those times.

Even at my most irrational, angriest times, you have to know that I loved you, Shay. I know you have always known that, and I take comfort in that. When I get out of this awful place, I'm going to be better – for myself, and for you. I won't be like these COs, taking out petty frustrations on those utterly powerless to defend against them. Despite their treatment of me, I'm not the animal they make me out to be… and what's more is that I refuse to become one. I take comfort in this, too. When I finally get out of here, I'll be better. Until next time…

Forever yours,
Sarah

Sarah Hendrickson 7278176
Maryland Correctional Facility for Women
7943 Brockbridge Road
Jessup, Maryland

May 3, 2006

Dear Shane,

I think one of the worst aspects of this place is the total disregard for individuality. Sometimes the things I would say or wear or do would lead you to look at me with that half-disbelieving look of yours. You know the look I'm talking about – that look that I love: head tilted to the side, eyebrows raised, eyes amused, mouth half-open in your goofy, signature grin. You would shake your head and remark "You really are your own person, aren't you?" Reality couldn't be further from that casual statement now. I'm no longer my own person; I belong to the Maryland Department of Corrections. I'm no longer Sarah Hendrickson; I'm 7278176.

They don't care. The guards see me as just another responsibility – an animal to be locked in her cage, to be uniformly clothed in the standard scratchy, threadbare jumpsuit, and to be let out for brief periods of exercise and showers. The state sees me as a danger to society: a serious criminal in need of serious punishment. They have found me guilty of an unthinkable crime, and they have locked me up and thrown away the key. The public *doesn't* see me — and somehow, this hurts even more. The message that I am no longer a part of society is received loud and clear. I am forgotten; banished to a cage to live a life that's not really mine — a life that's not really a life.

No one cares about the dynamic entity that was "Shane and Sarah" or the incredible love we shared. They don't care about the countless Sundays we spent cuddled together in our sweatpants watching football and ignoring the rest of the world. They don't care about the camping trips in the Poconos or our first time hang gliding in Costa Rica. They don't care. Together we had it all, and here I'm simply lost. What am I supposed to do now? Where do I go from here?

I miss you. Until next time…

Forever yours,
Sarah

On April 29, 2003, Shane Ryan Hendrickson was found dead in the kitchen of his home, the victim of 47 vicious stabbing wounds. The case concluded on November 3, 2003 when Sarah Alexandra Hendrickson, his college sweetheart and wife of 11 years, was found guilty of first-degree murder and sentenced to life in prison. While the evidence was largely inconclusive, the jury seemingly accepted the prosecution's depiction of Sarah as an unstable, cold-blooded murderer, finding her guilty largely due to, according to one juror, "the brutal nature of the murder and the lack of remorse and acknowledgement of responsibility on behalf of the defendant." Sarah continues to maintain her innocence, and continues writing letters to her late husband Shane every six months on the anniversary of her conviction.

The Day That Never Ends

By Zachary Faden

The day that never ends
Each hours passes
And repeats
And repeats
Continual twilight
Forever transition
Never another dawn
Only impending dusk
The words never spoken
Unformed whispers
Fighting formation
Mere expression exposes
Vulnerable and violated
Harshness hardens
Callous not callow
Expression and judgment
When the darkness comes.

An Offender in the Age of Innocence

By Zachary Faden

An offender in the age of innocence,
Bares a moral society's decadence.
The crime unquestionable,
But the response objectionable.
The slayer must be slain,
Must this edict be fain?
Does the obligation to justice
Mandate an act, loveless?
Can our craving for punishment
Be sated, while consistent
With empathy and redemption?
A pedagogical execution,
Simply teaches the future
All wounds must bleed, no suture;
Evil acts, a tumor, terminal,
Without treatment, only removal.

Bullied

By Rachel C. Cupelo

I remember that night.

I remember that night because it was cold, even for early April, even in the Adirondack foothills. It felt like it might snow, and a cloudy, pinkish night sky suggested as much.

I left my car by the side of the road that wound its way past the gorge, stepping onto the bridge and making my way toward the middle. The cold was damp, running through my coat, snaking its way into my veins and causing me to shiver violently.

I was already shaking for a different reason.

Even though the night was very dark, out here in the woods, I noticed someone already standing in the middle of the bridge, looking down at the rocky, icy streambed below. I was annoyed. I had something I had to take care of, something I didn't particularly want a witness to. I would have to bide my time, wait for him to leave the bridge.

"Hello," he said, as I walked up. He didn't take his eyes off the rocks below us.

I replied in kind, looping my arms around the thick iron bars that, being only chest-high, made merely the pretense of a human guardrail on the pedestrians-only bridge. I gripped so hard with my hands that some of the cheap industrial paint came off on my fingers in tiny green chips.

Suddenly, the guy next to me spoke up: "What are you doing up here anyway? It's two in the morning."

Once I listened to the voice again I realized that the man beside me was not a man at all, but a boy. I squinted a little because of the dark, but after a moment came to the conclusion that he must have been as young as I suspected – eleven years old, maybe twelve. A child. Why would a child be alone on a bridge at 2AM?

I answered his question with a small smile. "I could ask the same of you, kiddo."

"Don't call me kid. I'm not a kid."

They never thought they were. "So how old are you?"

"Fourteen. How old are *you?*"

Still young, but I wasn't quite correct. "I'm twenty. I'm a student at Ithaca College."

My slightly embarrassed, non-patronizing response seemed to mollify his petulance. He looked at me for another moment, studying me, as if trying to assess whether or not I was harmless. Having judged me accordingly, he sniffed, and stuck out his hand. "I'm Jack."

I returned the handshake. "My name's Danny."

"So what are you doing out here, Danny?"

I turned back to staring out into the trees. "Thinking."

"Same here."

But there was a catch in his voice, another sniff, a throat clearing. The light from the clouds shifted then, and I could just make out the tears coursing down his face.

"Not the same," I said. "What's wrong?"

"Nothing," he muttered, looking over the edge of the bridge again, deliberately avoiding my eyes.

"Not nothing. Tell me what's wrong. Maybe I can help." *One last good deed*, I thought to myself. *Why not?*

And then: "They hate me!"

I grabbed his arm, more forcefully than I intended, to make him look at me. "Who hates you?"

"They guys at school!"

"Tell me what happened."

"What usually happens! They beat me up, they spit on me, they knock my books out of my hands and kick me in the stomach when I get down to pick them up. They call me a queer and follow

me home and threaten to kill me! They wanna kill me because…"
he heaved a breath, "because…" And then the poor kid broke
down sobbing.

Without thinking, I grabbed Jack into my arms. I was
holding him too tightly, and I knew it, but the enormity of our
shared pain crashed into me then, knocking my breath out of me.

"…Because you're different," I finished for him.

He tried to wrestle out of my grip, and when I wouldn't let
go he just cried harder in frustration. "You don't get it! I'm not
just *different*," – he spat the word – "I'm EVIL, a walking sin."

He gasped for air. "I've tried so hard to just act NORMAL,
but they notice every detail – the way I walk, the way I talk, the
way I *cry*."

His sobs were heaving and dry now; he didn't have any air
left. I loosened my hold on him, placing my hands on his shoulders,
pushing him away just a little so he could look me in the eye.

"Listen to me, Jack. I *understand*."

He shook his head. He didn't believe me.

"But you…you're not – "

"It doesn't show. Sometimes it doesn't."

"Then how did you get caught?"

I let him go, gritting my teeth, turning back to the trees.
Tears burned behind my eyes and my voice cracked, despite my
attempt to keep it steady. The despair washed over me in another
massive wave. My knuckles were white where my hands gripped
the guardrail.

"I was stupid. I stopped being careful. I was just so *tired* of
it."

He didn't say anything, just looked at me, waiting for
more.

"Tired of looking over my shoulder, walking on eggshells,"
I muttered. "I was tired, and I slipped. We both did."

"We?"

"My boyfriend and I. We got careless. My roommate suspected, and I knew that, but I never thought…well, who knows what I thought."

The pain of the memory was unbearable, but suddenly the words came bursting forth, my rage and shame with them.

"He told me he was going to be at a party, so I invited Mark over. I just wanted to be with him, for a few minutes, without having to watch and listen constantly. I locked the door, and I thought we were safe. But my roommate was hiding in the closet with his camera. He takes a photography class, he has access to the processing labs at all hours. By the next afternoon, copies of the pictures were taped up in every hallway in every dorm, in the student lounge, the laundry rooms, even some of the classrooms. He's talented – you could tell exactly who we were and what we were doing."

I heaved a sigh. "That was five days ago. Mark disappeared; I heard he dropped out of school. I called his parents' place in Utica, but he won't return my messages.

"I tried to convince the dean and the school board that the pictures were fakes, but I don't think they bought it. The dean told me that if I agreed to be counseled by the school chaplain, that he'd consider keeping it off my record and out of hearing of my parents. I don't think he can really promise the latter, not with all those photos floating around."

"Damn." Jack had been silent before now, absorbing my story, but when I looked into his eyes, I realized that, for all his fourteen years, he understood the implications in every detail.

"What about your roommate?"

I smiled bitterly. "I overheard the dean commending him for exposing a *moral crisis*."

"That's terrible."

"It's exactly what I expected," I replied truthfully. "I have no idea what's going to happen now, but I have no desire to wait and find out."

Jack looked up at me expectantly, his eyes knowing.

"I'm jumping tonight." Saying it felt reassuring, final. But my voice broke again and I held back my tears with superhuman effort.

"I just can't wait around to find out what else they'll try to do to me, how they'll ruin my life."

Jack wasn't looking at me anymore, his eyes trained downward again, at the jagged rocks and rushing stream.

"That was my plan tonight too."

"I know. You couldn't wait around either."

His voice wavered, and he shook like a frightened dog. "They tried to hurt me yesterday, worse than usual. They cornered me in the locker room, beat me up, held me down, tried to rip my clothes off. They had an old mop handle they'd stolen from the janitor's closet. Who knows what else they planned on using. But I knew what would have happened if I hadn't escaped."

He took another heaving, shaking breath. "They told me that if I wanted to be a girl so badly, they'd treat me like one."

When he finally looked at me, tears were falling from his eyes again. "Next time they'll get me. I won't be able to escape. I can't wait around for that. I'd rather be dead."

"Won't anyone help?"

He shook his head. "Dad says I need to learn how to fight back. The principal told me I was being too sensitive, boys'll be boys, all that."

"I'm sorry, Jack."

He gave me a humorless smile. "I'm sorry too."

I saw the flash of metal and instinctively tensed, ready to hit the pavement if need be.

"Where the hell did you get that?"

He waved the revolver carelessly in the air. "Belongs to my dad. He'd kill me if he knew it was missing."

He read the fearful questions in my eyes, and I never had to ask. "I'd made my decision by last night about what I needed to do, but I was so *angry*, and I just wanted revenge. I wanted them to know what it feels like, to be terrified *every single goddamn DAY*! I want to take them out with me, because it's the very least of what they deserve."

I flinched momentarily when he spun the gun around his index finger and it almost dropped from his too-small, clumsy hands. "But you didn't. Why?"

"Because I'm a COWARD!" And then he was screaming, tears running down his cheeks, hysterical in a way that I wish I could muster, just for the temporary relief from the shame that coursed constantly through my being.

"I'm a coward!" he cried. "I brought it to school in my backpack, I musta had my hand in the bag and my finger on the trigger ten times, waiting for the right moment. But I couldn't! I couldn't do to them what they did to me!"

I shook my head. "That doesn't make you a coward, Jack. It makes you better than them."

He shook his head violently. "If I'd been any better than them, I would have just done it! Gotten rid of them, so that no one would ever have to feel MY PAIN! But I couldn't, and I know that if I wake up tomorrow I will go back there and I will actually do it. I'll kill every single last one of them. I know I won't be able to stop myself."

"So you figure that if you throw yourself over the bridge, you'll stop it, make it all go away?"

He nodded, wiping at his eyes. "If I go back there, either I kill them or they kill me. If I don't go back, I have to make the problem go away."

Jack looked up at me, his eyes begging me for something, I just wasn't sure what. "I'm out of choices, Danny. Can't you see that?"

Before I could reply, he pulled the hammer back and let the weapon rest casually across his chest.

"I'm probably too much of a coward to jump off this bridge, so maybe I should just take care of it right now."

It was stupid. I could have gotten myself killed. Of course, that had been the goal of the evening, and ten minutes before that moment I wouldn't have minded. It was just that, in the last ten minutes, my goals had changed.

I charged Jack, grabbed him by the wrist, and wrenched the gun from his hand. He didn't really fight back, and only gave me a slightly surprised look, almost as if he had expected and wanted it from me.

"Either I toss it or you do. It's up to you. Your *choice*."

He raised one eyebrow, mildly regarding my sudden aggression. "My father will kick my ass when he sees his gun is gone."

"The alternatives aren't any better."

He nodded in agreement at this, took the gun from me, and tossed it into the rocky, heavily forested streambed below. And then he stuck his hands in his pockets, rocked back on his heels, and took a breath, momentarily regretting his haste. Now he either had to die the hard way, or live, which was even more complicated.

It didn't matter. I knew what his decision would be, at least for tonight. Just as easily as he knew mine.

"Hey," I said softly, breaking the silence.

"What?"

"Where's your note?"

He looked at me questioningly.

"Your suicide note."

"Oh." He stuck his hand deeper in his left pocket, fishing out a ratty piece of loose-leaf paper, folded into a neat, tiny square.

"What about it?" he asked.

I took out my own note and grabbed a lighter from my coat, flicking it open and lighting it. The flame shot up a few inches before gradually dying down.

"There's this late-night diner down the road. I thought we'd grab an early breakfast." I said it casually, hoping he'd take me up on the offer, hoping that I could get us both out of there before we changed our minds again. All of a sudden it seemed absolutely necessary to leave the bridge and try, even if no good came of it.

He smiled, awkwardly, and nodded. Taking that as permission, I put my own note into the flame, holding onto the burning paper and holding out the lighter so that Jack could do the same. I saw that his hands were shaking as he held the very edge of the paper square to the flare, but when the flames jumped and almost burned the tips of his fingers, he grinned widely, dropped the paper, and stomped out the light with his shoe.

Having forgotten my own note, I did end up burning my fingers. Quite badly, actually. But it was worth it, to set fire to our pain and let the wind carry the ashes away. I let out an oddly cheerful cuss at the stinging in my fingers, and when I looked up again Jack and I locked eyes. Without a word, he took my hand, reaching up briefly to kiss my cheek, and then proceeded to pull me playfully toward my waiting car. I stopped him, pulling him into a final, crushing embrace, and after a few moments heard him whisper, very quietly, "thank you."

We pulled apart and kept walking. By the time we left the bridge, it had started to snow.

* * * * * * * *

I still remember that night, over forty years ago. It was April of 1968 in Upstate New York, and I met Jack on the bridge over the gorge near Ithaca College.

Jack and I stayed in touch for years after that night, even as we went off into the world and found all the things we needed that we couldn't get at home. I transferred and went to a school in New York City, and I was sitting in the Stonewall Inn when the riots began in 1969. With my grinning mug plastered all over the New York papers the next morning, my parents kindly requested I never set foot in their home again. So when I finished college a year later, I went off to California and spent a summer in Haight-Ashbury, basking in the liberty of anything-goes free love. I got my PhD and worked on Harvey Milk's campaigns and lived and loved, and I've never felt quite so free since. I went back to New York eventually, after Milk's assassination, reluctantly leaving my memories of Castro Street behind me. I became a professor, and met the love of my life in the West Village.

Jack disappeared for a few years, joining me in California during the middle of Harvey's third failed campaign, living in the shitty, roach-infested flat above mine on Castro, later following me to New York after everything had gone so badly.

Were we lovers? Sometimes, yes. But mostly no. You see, Jack had never truly recovered from what happened to him before that night on the bridge, and Milk's murder shattered him in ways I couldn't even fathom. I was familiar, a comfort, though after a while, not nearly enough. I never saw him with the same man twice, and I knew it was because he just couldn't force those memories from his mind, because every man reminded him of his torture, his shame and sin, and he never stopped believing that the next one would bring love and salvation.

It cost him. He died three weeks after his 30th birthday of Kaposi's sarcoma, brought on by a new disease they called the Acquired Immunodeficiency Syndrome. He certainly wasn't the only friend I lost during that time, but he is the one I remember most, not for his disease but for the pain that, even indirectly, led him there. He never got over what happened to him. Sure, we convinced each other to leave the bridge that night, but he was bullied until the day he left high school, and he never forgot a single shove, a punch, a threat, and certainly not the numerous attempts at rape in the locker rooms. He had nowhere to go, except back to that bridge, but he called me every single time he even thought about doing it, so that I could remind him that he had something to live for.

He just wanted love. He just wanted to be left alone. They wouldn't let him be happy, and the price was heavy.

Now, as I read and watch the news, I'm seeing it happen all over again. Over a dozen kids have died since the summer began, all because people weren't paying attention, or kept brushing it off, or punishing the victims for being vulnerable. And here I am, and I'm not a parent, and I'm not a teacher, but I am a survivor – I'm still here! – and I've seen so much change in the world since that night on the bridge.

But obviously, I haven't seen enough.

So here I am, and I don't know much of anything, but how to survive the aftermath of that pain. Here I am, an old queer, sitting in this even older easy chair, just trying to tell his story, not because my survival was miraculous or I was necessarily stronger than the rest and want to brag about it. I'm trying to tell you because, maybe, if you write this down, and send it out into the world, one less kid will think he's out of choices.

I couldn't be there for the kids that are already gone. I couldn't be there for Jack, not the way he needed. But I'm here now, having eased my guilt, and learned from my mistakes – having finally understood, despite my own story, that the pain doesn't end when the bullying ends – that the process of healing, of surviving, is a lifetime. Now knowing what I do, all I can think to say is that we're all in this together, whether we like it or not, so we better do something about it. If we don't, people are going to keep losing their children.

So do me a favor, and pass this story around. Don't do it for me, the old queer in the easy chair. I've managed my demons. But do it for Jack, and all the kids who died this year, all the people who feel locked up, their dignity and safety stripped of them by hatefulness and crime and victimhood. Let me be there for them this way, because all it takes is one encouraging word. Let me reach out and remind them that they are not alone.

It's true, I don't know much. But I do know what it means to be offered a glimmer of hope.

Please consider supporting The Trevor Project, or your local LGBTQ organization

Judgment Day

By Sonia Tabriz and Robert Johnson

Judgment Day came
Long ago
Life, the sentence
Death, the outcome

Jesus said
He who believes in me will live,
Even though he dies

And I did
Live
Though I was
Dead
To the world
Though I no longer
Believed

My soul starved
My body withered
Yet I endured
Trapped
In the coffin that is my cell
The tomb that is my tier

The gavel damned me to perdition
A living death
This penitentiary, my afterlife
After life on earth

The Wicked Quarter Mile

By James O'Brien

The plea was still scrawled across the far wall of my cell when they returned me four days after. A year and a half in lock up, I'd amassed a small collection of personal items that made me miss being a free human more than making me feel like one. All of that was gone. Along with the bed sheets, the lid to the hard blue steel toilet, pens, paper, and anything else I may hurt myself with. The bare bunk and toilet, my uniform and cream colored slip on shoes, and of course the remnants of my plea, etched about the far wall in the blood from my neck. I got the shiv from Woody Cooper, he was a nickel into a dime for theft, then he got a life extension for skinning the tattoo off another inmates chest. He hung it off his shoulder and walked perimeter like a caged animal with a badge of courage until the guards tackled him. It would have drove him nuts, the extended confinement, but in there he found himself a niche. He was the guy that got things, the procurer for all of C-Block. I'd never made a request of him before. I didn't smoke, hadn't done drugs since my arrest, thus I had nothing to offer up save for the six cents an hour I made cleaning the rectory and bathrooms. Cooper didn't want that, why would he? Six cents, a million dollars, all worthless in C-Block. When I told him why I wanted the shiv he looked at me a brief moment, his pale thin face gaunt and shallow about the eyes. We were in the yard; it was just after lunch, only a minute or two of free time left. He looked at me, studied me. I counted the breaths he took to pass the time. After a few of those breaths he nodded, a nod that said: No Charge.

Three days later Cooper slipped me a piece of chain link fence, six inches long, the top two inches filed down to a crude blade on his imported whet stone. And with that I slashed my own throat. Unfortunately the edge was too dull to get through the muscle, get to my jugular, either jugular. As the blood spilled I dipped my fingers into the laceration and plead my case about the far wall of the cell. A child painting rudimentary strokes, red against a hard white wash: *i give up let me have this freedom*. But, of course, they didn't.

What is freedom anyway? Freedom is unbreatheable air in prison, like being stuck in a smoke filled room – it must be inhaled even though it promotes no life. Four days in the infirmary. Suicide watch. Four more days in the infirmary after, while on suicide watch, I removed the bandage, tore out the sutures, and dug my fingers into the wound, trying to rip into the cord of veins. They wouldn't let me have it, though, my freedom. And now back to my cell. Empty of anything but the necessities of civilized confinement. I was now reduced to nothing, I had nothing. I had to agree with them. I would have done it again if given any chance.

* * * * * * * *

Eight months later. The three women wore identical green collard shirts with the same logo over their middle aged left breasts: Second Chances Of The West. We were in the adjunct office of Warden Wilson. Hard morning light collimated obliquely through the deep window cut well into the east wall. The women stood on one side of the light, I on the other. They presented smiles when I entered the room, smiles that held within them a modicum of effort. Smiles made by an uneasiness that has character one can only find in a prison. Something between fear, disgust, and pity. The warden had been there, moments before. I could smell the remnants of his cheaply rank after-shave. Jim Randy escorted me to the office from my cell. He was an alright man, for a gunbull. Truth be told he was better than alright, but he wasn't stupid, he was kind and he let his humanity seep out at appropriate times for appropriate inmates. He understood that not everybody in here was an animal. Some certainly were, and they deserved to be put down the way you put a sick animal down, and to them Jim Randy may as well have been the devil. But lucky for Jim he was in charge of C-Block, there weren't a hell of a lot of animals there. He was able to act like and treat men like human beings. I believe it made him happy.

In the office with the women Jim Randy stood close to my side the entire time. Not for me, though. A year ago, in a possible fit of boredom or temporary insanity, I guess I'd signed up for what the state penal system was calling their Special Programs. And now I had been chosen for one such program. I didn't really want it, then or now. But as with everything in lock up I didn't have a choice and I had to pay for my decisions. So, in the office with the three women; four and a half hours of orientation and training, including videos, lectures, and play-acting. I was walked back to my cell carrying a fifty pound bag of food in one arm and a five month old black lab named Fletcher in the other.

He was a sturdy dog of twenty-five pounds with coarse black hair that shimmered in sleek bands against the florescent blue lights of the corridor, like surface oil across pooled water. His eyes were quiet and attentive, arms and legs the antithesis. And he held the idea that everything in sight belonged in his goddamned mouth. I wasn't quite sure what they had just done to me, or, in reality, what I had just done to myself. Jim Randy locked us in my cage, went back to retrieve from the women two indestructible iron bowls. "Can't he just drink out of the toilet?" I asked as Jim turned away. He turned back and watched me through the bars for a long moment, his face bisected perfectly by a dull steel finger. He furrowed his brow, scratched his chin, "Don't make us regret doing this for you, okay?"

"*Doing this for me*, you call this a favor?" I asked, pointing down at the puppy, pissing all over the leg of my bunk.

"C'mon, Billy, you never had a dog when you were a kid?"

I leaned my tired forehead against the bars, closed my eyes. "You're a sweet fella for thinking I was a kid once."

"Oh shut the fuck up," Jim said, "stop being an asshole. Clean up that piss and try to appreciate something for once. If he pisses again, reprimand him, okay? Try to do it with your voice first, if you need to thunk him one on the head do it lightly, you don't gotta hit him. Try to use your voice because your hand should be a reward." Jim Randy walked away, listening, smiling for sure, as my soon screaming voice echoed off the concrete and steel.

* * * * * * * * *

I'd never had the nightmare before. Since I had tried to cut my own throat though, I'd been having this dream where I was alive forever, into some ungodly future where they just kept discovering ways to extend human. Everything changed but me. I just kept going as a clock never to die. The first time I woke up the puppy was on the floor, sleeping lateral and twitching himself in some wonderful dream of chase or feast. When I woke from the nightmare the second time, the puppy Fletcher was at the end of my bunk, again lateral, again twitching and paddling away in dreams. An hour later, the selfsame nightmare, and the puppy Fletcher now curled into my armpit. Another hour later, nightmare, and Fletcher sleeping again on the floor, by himself. Jim Randy came by my cell at first light, I was on the floor next to little Fletcher, his body warm and rhythmic with a depth of sleep that only the young can attain. I sat up. The puppy lifted his head a moment, looked up from me to Jim Randy, and then back down with closed eyes. "Well, ain't that something?" Jim said. "I knew you were a dog lover."

"What time is it?" I asked.

"Hour before Lights On." he said.

"Why?"

"You're going to leash train the little guy. Feed him a half bowl of that food there, I'll be back in forty five and we'll go out to the Quarter Mile, got it?"

I put a weak hand up to say sure, as if there existed a choice. He walked away nodding his thin haired head about his thick rolled neck. The nightmare left me sluggish and downright exhausted as we walked, forty-five minutes later, the three of us, to the Quarter Mile. Some of the lifers, the old timers, the institutionalized, the future, named this linear run of dirt the Wicked Quarter mile. Younger inmates simply called it the Quarter. One time some little MS-13 punk talked shit to a an old lifer, made a joke out of all of them thinking it held wicked, supernatural powers, like Mecca for the damned. They found him in pieces in the boiler room a week later. The old timers said, when asked why it was called such, they said it was your own reason. Everyone had their own reason for believing it wicked, or not. If it was meant to be then you'd find your own reason. That's what they said, anyway. It was the place to go exorcize whatever you needed to. The place you dealt with it. The place where you had that moment of clarity. At least that's what I took it to mean.

The three of us stood there at the head of the Quarter – Jim Randy, myself, and Fletcher the puppy. The sun was just below the granite horizon before us. Deep bands of dark blue, as if stroked by a mad god, stuttered across the lower sky. I yawned. Jim Randy yawned. Fletcher stood stout, ears erect, tail level with his head, pointing, and we could all hear the rock doves cooing in the early desert beyond. Jim looked over at the dog. "You might have lucked out, son."

"Why's that?" I asked.

"You got that dog leashed, sure, but still he isn't tear assing around, trying for them doves out there."

"Should he be?"

Jim Randy sighed, "Yes, Billy, he should be. He's a hunting dog, he's a puppy, and he's never been trained. Point being he's pretty well behaved."

"Maybe he's already been trained." I said.

Jim Randy studied the thinning clouds about the southern sky and adjusted his belt. "Doubtful. They found him somewhere down south, just a few weeks old, he had the parvo, they figured he'd die but...anyway, here he is. Okay let's knock off the bullshit and get something accomplished. I want you to make him sit, we'll start there."

"How come you're doing this with me and not the ladies from the organization?" I asked.

"I've had dogs my entire life."

"Yeah, so?"

"And them ladies was scared of you."

I looked down at Fletcher, still erect and focused one hundred percent on the birdcalls beyond. "Scared of me, huh?" I, for whatever reason, despised knowing that. Never in my life have I wanted to hurt anyone.

"Well, you got that big old scar across your throat."

"Yeah?"

Jim Randy looked at me, "Well, Bill, they read your file. *That big old scar* you did to yourself. Guess it spooked 'em a little."

"Right, but *I* did it to *myself*."

"Billy, it's abnormal. It's sick. They train dogs. That's all they know how to do, that's all they care about."

"Why didn't they train this one?"

Jim Randy walked a few steps away from me, rubbing the back of his neck red, his sign of annoyance. "Goddamn it…" He toed the dirt at his boot tip, turned to face me. "Fighting life all the time ain't a way to know you're living. Even in here."

"There is no way to know you're alive in here, Jim. You know that."

"Bullshit. You're a fuckin' coward."

I began to open my mouth but Jim Randy cut me off, "Yeah, yeah, so you cut your own throat, so you would've gone all the way if you'd of had a sharper shank. So the fuck what? That doesn't prove that you used to be here, on earth, be it in prison or not. Death ain't proof, you fuckin' idiot."

"Then what is?"

"Hell, I dunno…start with that, right there. That little goddamn dog you're giving a second chance at life. He was about to be put down, now he's not, because he's got a foster: you. And you're going to make him a good animal for a good home. Just start there. Christ almighty, for a person that claims to not give a shit about his life you're really taken with yourself, you know that? Prove to me that you don't have to be. Fuck that, prove it to yourself."

The morning dove flew off. Fletcher stayed put. The sun was just fixing to burst over the tops of the granite peaks surrounding us. Locusts blew. The desert was quiet. He was right, it was an act, that's why I said nothing. Seldom is it easy to admit when someone else is right, at least for me. I looked at Fletcher sitting at my side, ears still attentive, as if waiting for something, anything, and waiting for it from me. The sun dusted the loose clouds a furious pink. Jim Randy was watching me, himself waiting.

There are times when you keep your mouth shut, and even though it tastes like bile it's the best thing you may have ever done. Better people call it taking your medicine.

"Alright, what do I do?" I asked.

There is no debate in lock up. No debate. No choice. Really, no life. The day is mapped out with the simplicity of breath, action and reaction. It can be stripped down to wake up, eat, stand around, eat, go to sleep. There is no room for deviation. Until they let you have a dog. Then you are something bigger than a number, a routine, something bigger than even yourself, which is all you've known for so long. You truly realize Jim Randy was right and then, once Fletcher is asleep next to you, you deal with the pain of too little too late. Some nights when shadows run long of the cell and you hear distant men crying as if the dark hides sound, you wish for ignorance. You wish you'd never seen the dog. Never heard the words of Jim Randy playing half assed preacher or therapist, because then once again you are reminded not of life, but of this life. A life of inert and motionless possibilities, which in reality are impossible. A stagnant repetition of breath and day and night. A life where you are no longer privy to even the basic elements, only their modified leftovers of steel and mortar. You wait for an outlet that will never come in a super max facility. That's when you begin searching for one. Here's the outlet I found:

Three weeks later Fletcher was basic in his skills, a little behind the rest of the group, but that was my fault for granting him leeway on his instincts. The rest of the group, whom we were meeting for the first time this particular morning, was a small pack of four other dogs all living with their trainers in A-Block, minimum security, white collar fellows. In fact I was the only one below A-Block to participate in this program. We met in the second rec yard, A-Block's yard, just after breakfast. They were mostly working dogs in the group, labs and a pointer, but also one mutt with a chronic nervous face. The grass was fresh cut, still wet with drops of sprinkler water. Fletcher was jerking so hard at the leash I just let him have it. He took to pissing about everything in mad circles about the yard. Jim Randy was suddenly yelling, "Get that goddamn dog back at your side!" And I forestalled, hands in pockets, until Randy realized yelling didn't do anything. He walked Fletcher back to me, shoving the leash end into my hand. "The fuck is the matter with you?" he asked lowly. I shrugged my shoulders, said nothing. The socialization exercise lasted just over an hour, supposed to be ninety minutes but I attacked one of the A-Block inmates. In seconds I'd found my outlet. He was the one training the mutt, some kind of Shepard lab mix, brown with a giant head and calm, if not sort of dumb, disposition. He strayed from his trainer who thought himself more a master. The guy jerked the chain back towards himself, glanced over his shoulder and, seeing that Jim Randy and the other guard were with another inmate, he smashed the dog on the head with full fist of clenched fingers. As he was raising his fist I saw the mutt cower, he knew what was coming and in his calm, if not dumb, manner he tried weakly to not accept it. But what could he really do aside from running the end of his leash taught? I stood from the humid grass where I'd been sitting with Fletcher, he and the pointer had been pawing at one another, chewing on ears and tails. He stood and sat as I rose up, ignoring his playmate. I ran a palm coat-wise down his black, hot, head. "Sit." I asked. He did. "Stay." He did. I handed Fletcher's leash tip to the pointers quiet trainer, said not a thing. The mutt did nothing as I beat his owner into the grass. His jaw fractured. One punch after another. Eye sockets gave way. He bit part of his tongue off. I somehow got my knuckles to rip his ear half off.

And just like that my outlet was no longer needed, replaced with something else. And that was this: lying prone with Jim Randy's knee in my back, zip tying my wrists, I pushed my sweat damp head up. Across the yard there was Fletcher, still sitting, pink tongue dripping out of the side of his panting mouth, attentive only to me. I figured that would be the last time I'd ever see him. I closed my eyes and stuffed my face in the damp grass so nobody would see the wetness of my eyes.

* * * * * * * * *

"You out of your fucking mind?" It was Jim Randy, though I couldn't see him. They'd put me in isolation. Lightless, like a deep cut trench at the bottom of the ocean, void and silent, capable of driving men mad. But not me. Not now. I welcomed it. Self-punishment for self-abuse. The second of the two security doors hung open, a trail of washed out florescent light, a fallen stanchion, came about and bisected the blackness. I sat in the corner, the edge of my shoe visible weakly in the column. Jim Randy was in the room, disappeared somewhere in the darkness. "You don't have to answer that." he said, "It doesn't really matter." I listened to him sigh greatly. "But…I will say, you lucked out."

"Oh yeah?" I asked, pushing myself up against the cold mortar wall that I imagined a steel blue color. The light column dimmed to eventual nothing as the outer door closed with unforeseen gravity. "How so?"

"Me. You get to keep the dog. You have to stay in here another twenty four hours, but, you get to keep training the dog." he said. His voice was soft, echoing as a ping-pong ball back and forth. We were two jet-black bats communicating in some ancient neolithic cave. "Unless you don't want to." he said. I kept my eyes closed because, as I was telling myself, the column of light burned them to tears. In the hollow silence, devoid of anything but breath, an electrical sense of somatic want became me. I wanted Fletch right there. I didn't need food or water. I didn't even need vision. I needed my companion for the blackness. My outlet had come and gone and was nothing more or less than before. It was the same as dope use and it's even less cathartic. In that darkness I just didn't know if I could ever keep from fooling myself. This was an automatic disposition I often took at times like this. Better people call it feeling sorry for themselves. I never called it that, until I was there in that darkness, until I was without something that was better, more important, than myself.

* * * * * * * * *

I continued to train Fletcher for the next eleven months. His training, though, only took about six months. The next five were spent simply being his owner, his friend, whatever I was to him. *His* companion. His progress was picked up by a young family that lived down state somewhere. They followed his training and socialization, they wrote often and requested photos. I took the pictures, I was never in them. The eleventh month found me in my cell and the three women from the organization standing before my cage. I knew what came next. I scratched his ear as he sat at my feet leaning his head into the scratch, shoving his head into the scratch. His dark eyes – squinted with the integrity of well felt contact – bounced flippantly between me and the women. My heart was pounding. I felt nauseated. My legs refused to rise from the edge of the bunk. He placed his paw clumsily on my knee, his freshly trimmed nails scratching at the fabric of my pant leg. My throat welled sickly. An hour later he was gone.

That afternoon I was outside, raking the rocks at the Quarter Mile. The sun bleated pulsing rays of heat as I began, a celestial convection oven, threatening and nurturing all at once. By the time I finished the giant star was drowned behind a cell of metallic gray thunderheads that may as well have come from nowhere, for the sky was wicked blue when I started, wicked gray and electric when I finished. I raked over paw prints in the loose dirt, whether they were really Fletch's or not I couldn't say. I felt the phantom limb of his muzzle against the edge of my palm. And suddenly the Quarter Mile, wicked as it was, became the only place I wanted to be.

* * * * * * * *

Later Jim Randy came by my cell. "Sucks, huh?"

I said nothing. He adjusted his belt, the taught leather strap crunching freshly beneath his muffin top gut. He rested his hands through the space in the bars, as he often did. He was chewing gum and he looked up the corridor, down. "Never gonna be easy." he said. I nodded along, laying supine about my thin bunk. He knew I knew that, for guys like me some things just need to be put out there in the audible atmosphere. He glanced above my head momentarily, "Looks like Fletch tried to lick your little blood journal off the wall, huh?" I nodded again, the presence of the old blood streaks like bits of paint flesh, present and gone at the same time. They'd given me sheets and a toilet seat again. I refused anything else, collectibles or possessions, color or character.

Jim pushed himself off the bars, hands on hips, studying his well polished boot tips. I was waiting for him to chastise me about the lack of decor, lack for want of humanity in a place like this. But he never did. And later that evening I think I knew why. "The program starts again next month." he said. "You ready for the next one?" And despite my weakening instinct to say Fuck you, or just nothing at all, I said yes. Truth was I couldn't wait.

Empty Cell Windows

By Sonia Tabriz[1]

Adapted for the Stage by Ellen W. Kaplan

> (A bare stage. Only one set piece
> is needed – a partition that
> demarcates outside from inside.
> This could be a screen, or a line of
> chairs; an empty doorframe
> through which 'outsiders' pass
> would be best. SOPHIA stands at
> the door; the GUARD sits)

GUARD

Alright, ladies.   Everyone's out.

SOPHIA

What...? Who?

GUARD

The men. They're out.

SOPHIA
(backs away from the door)

How did they get *out*?

---

[1] Empty Cell Windows, written by Sonia Tabriz, was first published in
Tacenda Literary Magazine; a slightly revised version was reprinted in
Lethal Rejection: Stories on Crime and Punishment (Carolina Academic
Press, 2009: 143-145)

GUARD

You can go in. They're ready for you. C'mon, sweetheart, we don't have all day here.

SOPHIA
(to audience)
I think, you certainly *do* have all day. But after my momentary panic when he said the men were 'out' – *on the loose?* I thought. *Aren't they dangerous?* – well, after that, I figured I'd better not go making wisecracks.

GUARD
(droning on, it's a boring routine)
Sign your name, empty your pockets, leave your belongings in the lockers, no wallet, keys, cell phone, pen, coins, cameras. Don't give anything to anyone at any time. Step through here please, *thank* you, next.

SOPHIA

Five of us. Students. Girls. One by one. Here we go…Inside.

STUDENT #2

This is like, wow, like my very first time in *prison,* you know?

GUARD

Alright, *ladies.* Stop your chatter. You're in prison.

SOPHIA

He means, this isn't a theme park. This is real.

GUARD

Let's go, this way.

SOPHIA

And we do it. One by one.

STUDENT #2
(to SOPHIA)

This is it.

SOPHIA

Pass through the metal detector.

STUDENT #2

We're going inside.

SOPHIA

Into the visitation area.   That's where I see….the boy.

            (SOPHIA steps away from the
            doorframe.
            A YOUNG BOY is sitting alone
            on a chair. HE
            stares into the distance. SOPHIA
            watches him.)

SOPHIA
(to us, as she watches the boy)

He looks so young. Thirteen or so.   The lines of his face are soft,
innocent. He's here with his mother, I guess she's his mother.   For
a moment he looks at me, vacantly.   His gaze is hollow, his eyes are
sad.   Who is here to see? I'd like to ask him. But I don't.

GUARD

Keep walking please.

SOPHIA

That boy. His face stays with me. Who does he have inside?   I will
look for a face that resembles his…here. In the cellblock. In max.

GUARD

Okay, ladies. Welcome to Maryland Correctional Adjustment Center. Now, when we go into the cellblock, I want you to remember where you are. This is a <u>maximum-security prison</u>, *super max!* They might get rowdy, might shout obscenities or what, but you just ignore them. Walk through cool and calm, alright? You're perfectly safe, just don't talk , keep on moving, you'll be fine.

STUDENT #2

Are they all in their cells?

GUARD

Yes ma'am.   Right this way.

SOPHIA

We walk through a heavy metal door leading into cellblock AD-307; the number is on the door of what looks like a command center. Then into a long, narrow hallway.

GUARD

This here glass partition separates the inmates' cells from the guards.

STUDENT #2

Are those the cells? Behind this glass?

GUARD

Yes, ma'am. Bulletproof glass.

SOPHIA

Locked metal doors.

SOUND: Prison doors slamming;
men's voices shouting

GUARD

Safely behind bars.

INMATE
(calling out)

Hey. Yo. Mamma! Gimme something hot!

GUARD

Good thing too.

SOPHIA

We walk.   Most of the men are inside. I can't see them.   But some look out their cell windows. (BEAT) I don't see them either – I am unable to look them in the eye.

GUARD

Some of these guys are gonna be rowdy, don't let it bother you. They don't get many visitors, these guys.

SOPHIA

Some whistle, some curse, some are quiet. I try to look at their faces. I want to find a trace of the boy's face. Who does he come to visit in here? Father? Brother? I don't find a resemblance anywhere. No one I see has his eyes.

INMATE
(shouting, from shower stall)

Hey! You in college?

STUDENT #2

Look, that bald guy.   He's in the shower stall!

INMATE IN SHOWER
(con't, shouting)

You in high school?

STUDENT #2

Why is he so angry.

SOUND:

Pounding on metal shower
stall.

INMATE IN SHOWER
(aggressively)

I'm talking to you!

SOPHIA

None of us answered him.

INMATE IN SHOWER
(banging on the shower stall)
You from anywhere? Where the f*k....?

SOPHIA

I thought about answering....

GUARD
(to inmate in shower)
Alright, cut it out. Move along, ladies.

SOPHIA

But I turned my back and walked away.

STUDENT #2
(*giggles nervously*)
Do you think we should talk to them?

SOPHIA
(to Student #2)

I'd like to....

STUDENT #2

Don't! I mean…ooohh. Maybe it's not a good idea.

SOPHIA

That bald guy, in the shower, I was going to….

STUDENT #2

He was so angry! He's probably some kind of rapist, or murderer
or something….

GUARD

These men have violent histories. You shouldn't invite contact in
any way.

                                                    SOUND: Men's

vcices, indistinct,
            calling: *Eh, puta? Not gonna eat*
                            you. Come over here. Talk to me!

SOPHIA

We walk. And slowly, I lift my eyes – I begin to notice *their* eyes.
A dark forest of eyes peering through the tiny windows of their cell
doors. I'm in a dark forest, the kind you read about in a children's
book; eerie owl eyes pierce the night. Owl eyes. Staring *out* from
tiny windows. And faces. Fragments of faces, all sizes, shapes and
colors. Behind cell windows. (BEAT) Then I realize, what I am
drawn to – more than the eyes in the windows – are the empty
spaces. The empty windows. Whose eyes *aren't* there? (BEAT)
Don't the men inside those windows want to look out at *me?*

INMATE IN SHOWER

Eh, puta!

                                                    SOUND:

Banging on shower stall.

SOPHIA

Yes, his cell is empty; *he's* in the shower. But the others? Empty windows that remain clear of all curiosity.

STUDENT #2

Like, you'd think they'd *want* to see five pretty girls, right? I mean, are those cells just empty or what?

SOPHIA

No, these cells aren't empty. These men simply choose not to look.

                                        SOUND: Owls hooting in the forest.

SOPHIA

But why? Hidden in the dark forest, this forest of cement. Whose eyes can't I see? Who is behind those windows?

INMATE A

I am. Drowning in sadness.

INMATE B

I am. Talking to the walls.

INMATE C

Longing for love I never had.

INMATE D

Keepin' cool til I burst out in a hopeless rage of fire. .INMATE

INMATE E

Scrubbing and scrubbing, scrubbing the floors to get rid of the roaches. I am.

INMATE F

Adorning the walls with my own shit.

SOPHIA

The ones I can see – with their wide yellow eyes, owl eyes peering
out. I can be ready for them. But it's the eyes I can't see that
frighten me. The unknown – the absent eyes – that make me feel
afraid. The unknown leaves you terrified. These empty windows –
these are the dark niches of my forest. I want to know who's
inside, before they're swallowed by the dark.

GUARD
(to SOPHIA)

You wanna *what?* Alright, but you crazy. Nobody sane asks to sit
in a cell, all by themselves.

SOPHIA

The guard thought I was mad, but he put me inside just as I asked.
It didn't take long inside that cell before I started to *go* mad. *(her
voice changes, she is increasingly agitated, breathless)*

    Where to look, into the corners, into the dark. Infestation.
Bugs.

(normal voice)

    In the cell for just moments, and going mad.

(agitated again)

    Scrub the floor, stare at the walls. Stale air, rancid smell.

(normal voice)

    Incantations to drive away the terror. I was already starting
to feel

(agitated)

Immobilized. Paralyzed. Terrified.

(normal voice)

There was nothing to distinguish day from night. There is
nothing…
And finally I started to feel…. *Indifference.   Utter apathy.*

Who is inside those empty cell windows? What is their life like,
these men I can't see? Here I am, in Cell 97, staring out with owl
eyes in the forest of steel cages and cement blocks. Staring at those
empty cell windows.

GUARD

Had enough?

SOPHIA

The guard unlocks the door.

GUARD

Time to go.

SOPHIA

And the thick cellblock doors snapped shut. (BEAT) As we leave, I
look for a face that resembles that little boy in the waiting room. In
none of the fragmented faces do I see even a shadow of the soft
innocence I'd seen in the boy. These faces, what I see of them, are
stripped of innocence. Stripped of everything that makes them
human.

GUARD

Well, ladies. There are some deep-rooted problems here. As you
see.

STUDENT #2

Deep-rooted problems. Yeah.

SOPHIA

And we left.

STUDENT #2
(to SOPHIA)

Did you see that boy before? I wonder who he was here to see.

SOPHIA

Left them behind.

STUDENT #2

I guess he's gone.

SOPHIA

Inside. Behind empty windows.

A Night in the Drunk Tank

By William Roth

When Brad knocked, Oliver opened the door to his apartment. Other people including Cil and Waring were already there. Somebody he did not recognize played a guitar and sang. Incense flavored the air. Glancing up from where she sat as part of a circle of people on the floor, Cil smiled weakly. Waring's guitar lay in his lap but he was not playing. He looked up, then looked away again without any change of expression.

Coming out of the bedroom, Carl, the young man Oliver sometimes allowed to stay in his apartment, waved listlessly. He was dressed in his usual patched dungarees and Mick Jagger tee shirt. After looking around to see who was there, Carl turned, went back into the bedroom as Brad settled himself on the floor at a right angle to Cil and Waring so he would not be facing them. A few minutes later Carl wandered out of the bedroom again. Stepping into the middle of the circle he put down a plate covered by crumpled tin foil on which lay a loaded hash pipe and crumbs of chopped up hashish. He did not say anything. He just moved out of the circle again, slumped into an easy chair and stared blankly up at the ceiling.

When Brad walked into the kitchen to get some wine Cil followed, watching uneasily as he took a glass down from the rack. "…So, what's been happening in your life?" Her voice sounded uncertain. Peering closely he saw that her face was drawn, dark crescents hanging under her eyes. Cil smiled sadly. "I guess that's not the right thing to ask." When he reached to put his hand on her cheek, to touch the glossy black hair that broke over her shoulders she blocked it with her own in mid-air. "Please don't."

"Is there anything I can do, Cil?"

"No." She shook her head, "I wish we could spend time together, but that wouldn't work right now."

"How's Waring?"

"He still won't talk to me."

When they reentered the living room Waring watched carefully until Cil was seated again beside him. Oliver squatted in front of Brad, "I'm glad you could come. Your ex-wife might show up later on. I told her you would probably be here. She said that would be all right. It would be pretty hard for the two you to continue avoiding each other."

A soft knock sounded at the door. Oliver leapt up. "That might be her now."

"Oliver?" A male voice inquired from outside. Oliver's face took on a puzzled expression as he cracked the door open to look out. Then he leaned hard against it, trying to force it closed but was thrown stumbling backward into the corner as the door exploded off its hinges.

"COME ON! COME ON!" A squat pee jacket barreled through the opening almost tripping over Brad before regaining his balance. Another man with a holstered pistol on his belt entered quickly.

Then a well built blond crew-cut wearing khakis and a blue sweatshirt stepped casually through the empty door hole, stood looking around to see who was there. "Hello, Waring."

Waring coughed, "Hello, Officer Ballard."

"What is going on here, Waring?"

"A party, Officer Ballard."

"Where's Oliver?"

"Here I am." Oliver stepped forward from the corner rubbing his shoulder.

"What's going on here, Oliver?"

"A party, Officer Ballard."

"Do you mind if I look around?"

"Do you have a search warrant, Officer Ballard?"

"No."

"Then I would prefer that you do not look around."

"I can leave men here, go back and get one."

"That's fine, Officer Ballard. Then you may look around."

The other agents moved slowly through the room fingering the leaves of plants, running their hand behind books on the shelves.

One examined an antique table lamp, flicked it on, off. He stopped for a moment in front of a Durer print, "Did you see this, Ted?" Then he carefully lifted the frame away from the wall, looked behind it.

Brad took a deep breath trying to clear the light-headedness he felt. Waring's knee jiggled. The pipe and hashish lay in the middle of the circle. Everybody stared, withdrawn, down at the floor except for Cil, who watched Brad.

"The host here says all they've got is beer and wine." Ballard smiled conspiratorially at his associates. "I would really like your permission to look around. Oliver."

"I would insist that you secure a search warrant first, Officer Ballard."

"Well, actually, I'm allowed to look around without one, so long as I don't move things." Stepping into the circle, he stooped over the pipe and the hashish, examined them with mock curiosity. "And what is this, Oliver?" When no answer came he turned to one of his men, "Officer Perse, what do you think this is? You've had training in identification."

"Looks like hashish to me, Officer Ballard."

"In that case you all are under arrest for possession of narcotics. Stand up and lean against the wall."

While the other officers went through everyone's pockets Officer Ballard read them their rights, then asked, "Everybody ready to go? Got everything you came with?..."

When they reached the police station Oliver asked permission to make a phone call. Officer Ballard said, "Later. Get this done first."

While the desk sergeant took the necessary information Chief Comley walked in wearing civilian clothing. He talked to Officer Ballard, then stood examining the group from across the office. Several minutes later the chief left.

Oliver asked again, "Officer Ballard, may I make a phone call?"

"Soon as we get everybody locked up."

The women were sent upstairs with a matron. Cil glanced

back at Brad before she disappeared. The men were led to a large, rectangular cage of bars housing six smaller, doorless cells that faced onto a narrow walkway. Ballard opened the gate. As they filed through Oliver hesitated, "May I make my phone call now?"

Shoving him in, the officer slammed the cage door shut. "That phone call stuff is just in the movies, Oliver. Didn't you know that? We don't have to let you make a phone call." Smiling, the officer stood watching their discomfort for several minutes, then turned away, walked back out into the office closing the glass-paneled door behind him.

While the others mulled about in the open space just inside the cage door Brad escaped down the narrow passageway. Two of the cells were occupied by older men with stubble beards; stained clothes; corroded, blotched skin. One was lying on the flat sheet of steel hanging by chains from the back wall of his cell. He had thrown up. As Brad watched, he rolled into the vomit. The other man leaned toward Brad, "You carry cigarettes on you?"

"No."

"I gotta get me a cigarette." The man shuffled hesitantly around the cell inspecting the slime caked floor. Bending over, hanging onto a bar for balance he dug one butt out of the crud, than another. "…Gotta get me a cigarette." Tearing two sheets of toilet paper from the role sitting in the corner he doubled them over, smoothed them out on the steel bed with shaking hands. Then the man opened the butts, dumped their contents onto the toilet paper. Some of the tobacco was soggy, clumped. He shredded it between blackened fingers. When it was loose, he shaped the tobacco carefully into a ridge down the center of the sheet, then rolled a cigarette, licking it to make it hold together. Digging a stick match from his pocket, he struck it, but could not hold the fire to the end. Finally, bracing his shaking hand against a bar, he leaned the cigarette into the flame.

While puffing hungrily, trying to keep it going, the old man closed his eyes. A puddle of urine began to form on the cement floor at the bottom of his left pants leg. He did not seem to notice, hanging onto a bar for support; hanging onto life now only because it had become a habit…As Brad watched he wondered why hopeless people like these bothered him so much? Was it because he saw something of himself in them; that things would not work out, that things would never work out no matter how hard he tried, so that eventually he to would give up, like these men had given up, and spend the rest of his time waiting to die, feeding the emptiness inside with alcohol or dope…

Brad grimaced. And that was really stupid. That didn't make any sense at all…Though as he watched the old man smoke his soggy cigarette the uneasiness would not go away, though he knew somehow that this man was not a total stranger to him…

Brad walked on down the passageway. Picking an empty cell he lay flat on the bunk feeling the cold dejection of steel soak up through his shirt and pants into his flesh. He stared at the uncompromising bars above, the bars on either side, the bars, bars, bars. His eyes dragged across bars, plucked numbly at bars, strummed down bars rasping out a dead tone that crashed to the cement floor, then clambered back up. He saw a symmetrical pattern of bars, a perfect cage of bars and felt trapped again. But this time he knew that escape was impossible. No matter how much he wanted to, no matter how much he was willing to risk, he could not get up and leave, he could not walk out the door. Not this time…

Wiping his brow, he realized he was sweating. A draft of hot air from the square, industrial fan mounted on the ceiling blew down over him. He needed to think about something else…Think about Cil. She had stared at him during the bust and again as the women went up the stairs. Cil had stared at him as though he were the one who could do something…

Wandering into his cell, Waring said, "So it finally happened. They finally got us."

"Yes."

"If Oliver hadn't opened the door so quickly…" Waring bent his head, growled, "They're going to break me. They're just going to keep hammering away until they finally break me. They never stop." He slammed his open hand against the bars.

"We have to stay calm, Waring."

Oh, that's great!" Waring spun angrily, "That is just great! Thanks for the advice, Brad. That's just what I need from you, advice on how to handle myself. Now, perhaps, you can also give me advice on how to save my marriage? Do you want to give me advice on that, too?"

Brad lay silent.

"…They came and got Oliver. I think they're trying to make some sort of deal with him."

"So now we're criminals."

"I guess so," the slow drawl hung heavy with sarcasm. "I guess that's what these bars mean." Walking away, Waring shook his head, "Yes, sir, I guess that's what these bars mean. Good observation, Brad, very good…"

Closing his eyes, Brad tried to shut his mind down. Immediately his other senses grew more acute. The chill from the metal beneath his back, the whir of the fan spewing hot air from above, the damp odors of mold and urine. He opened his eyes again, looked around. The only irregularity in his cell was a rusted hole about eight inches wide in the bottom back corner. This must have been where prisoners urinated before the toilet had been installed in the passageway. Standing, he left his cell, walked past the others. Each had a rusting hole in the same spot, thousands of small streams burning through the iron baseboard.

Carl lay by himself in a cell staring upward.

Forcing a smile, Brad said, "I guess we did it this time, eh?"

The boy's expression did not change. He did not answer.

"We'll be all right, Carl."

The boy spoke quietly, "When I was younger and my mother got drunk and beat me out of the house so she could be alone with her boyfriends I used to walk the streets. They would arrest me, put me in here to give me a place to sleep as much as anything. One night a man hung hisself, one of the drunks. He tore strips out of his pants and hung hisself while I was in here. He was too heavy. I was too small to lift him down. I tried to pull him down. He gurgled, made all sorts of strange noises. I yelled. But they ignored me. Nobody came. I yelled for an hour before somebody finally walked back to see what was going on. He just hung there, spinning slowly, all sorts of things dribbling down…"

"Well, you're not alone this time, Carl. You're with friends. We'll get you out of this."

Lurching upward onto his elbows, the boy snarled, "Everybody's alone, man! Don't go handin' me that 'you are with friends' crap! I've heard it too many times before. Everybody's alone, man! Everybody's got to take care of hisself as best he can! They said they would put me in jail and throw away the key because I had done some dealing! They said that if I didn't…" The boy stopped suddenly.

"Didn't what, Carl?"

But instead of answering, the boy rolled over onto his stomach, buried his head in his arms.

Hearing the gate open, Brad turned to see Oliver reenter the cage. The narrow shouldered man stopped just inside, his lips pursed, a frown on his face, staring back toward where Carl lay.

Waring walked up to him, "What did they want?"

"It doesn't matter," Oliver shook his head, "They didn't get it."

"Did they let you make a phone call?

"No, but Cil's father arrived. He is out there now arranging bail. He's already hired a lawyer…"

Integration

By Franziska Kabelitz

Once
I traveled to a just place
where my voice would be heard
and my presence welcomed.
Where I was safe.
Free.
Happy.

Once
I traveled to a distant place
where my ideas would fly
and my work shine.
Where my children were born.
Raised.
Married.

Once
I traveled to a cold place
with a fence around my house
and envied by friends.
Where memories determined life.
Language.
Success.

Once
I traveled to a just place
where law ruled society

and society ruled my home.
Where I drowned in chaos.
Hope.
Return.

At least
I traveled.
Once

No Outlet, Dead End

By Laury A. Egan

Gerald Garko fell backward, his hands clawing wet grass. "Holy shit!" he cried. Stunned, he stared at the sight of the bloody body lying half in the lake, then flipped over and frantically scrambled up the slope, his fingers grabbing trees and bushes, anything that would hasten his escape. At the top of the embankment, Gerald hesitated, as panic pierced his chest like spears. Although he wanted to run, Gerald coveted the road bike that stood in front of him—a titanium, Merlin Extralight model— brand new, its bronze frame glowing in the October sun. Gerald didn't know whose it was, but its front tire was flat. He thrust his

right arm through the frame, hoisted the bike diagonally onto his shoulder, cursing the oil staining his blue fisherman's shirt, and ran toward the main street of Stardust Lake.

It was 9:00 on a Saturday morning. There weren't many cars on Lakeshore Drive, one of the town's two perpendicular thoroughfares, the other being Lakeside Drive. Anxiously, Gerald checked behind him, hoping no one would see where he was coming from. He knew stealing the bike could cause serious trouble, but nothing compared to what had just happened.

As the front tire twisted sideways, Gerald wrestled with it, all the while walking as fast as he could, his sneakers slapping the pavement, left-right, toes pointing out like a duck. Everyone teased him about his feet. Hell, everyone in high school teased him about everything. He hated most of the kids, except for Hawk McKenny, his best friend, who was half Huron Indian and half a bunch of other things like Portuguese, English, and Czech. After this morning, though, Hawk and he probably wouldn't ever hang out again.

At Willow Street, Gerald turned right and kept close to the grove of trees. Larry Wreblewski, who was mowing crabgrass in his front yard, saw him.

"Shit!" Gerald muttered to himself.

Although most everyone in Stardust Lake was either intermarried or related — Larry was second cousin to Gerald's mother — they didn't like each other, so there was no reason to stop and talk. Gerald kept walking the last half-mile to his house.

The Garko home was a silver trailer with plywood extensions tacked on its south side. Pink insulation peeked between rotting wood, and water pipes ran here and there wrapped in newspaper. Between the two wings, a platform composed of knobless doors set side by side was wedged in. This was where his family socialized in decent weather, sitting on folding chairs and a plaid vinyl couch while staring out on the lawn, a patch whose weeds and grass had lost the battle for supremacy to the junk and beer cans. In the midst of the chaos sat a 1957 pink-and-white Mercury Montclair Phaeton Sedan, its butt twisted up on a cinderblock, its nose pointing toward the house like it was cruising into its final resting place, which Gerald figured it had, since it was unlikely his father would find four tires and all the parts for the car. Behind the Merc, the space where his dad parked his Ford 150 truck was empty. Gerald heaved a sigh from deep within his lungs. The old man was either at work or holding down a barstool — pretty much interchangeable occupations since his father worked for a beer distributor.

Relieved he only had his mother to contend with, Gerald stashed the road bike behind the propane gas tank and covered both with a scrap of frayed electric-blue tarp. Rubbing his oily hands together, he noticed blood on his palms and the sleeves of his shirt. He had to clean the stains off, but how could he sneak into the bathroom without his mother spotting the blood? She filled up half the trailer, her 400 pounds of flesh socked into the loveseat that fitted her like a single chair. He opened the screen door, took off his navy beret, and hid his hands inside its enclosure.

"Hi, Ma," he said, cutting in front of the TV set, which was blasting a quiz show. Canned laughter and on-cue clapping reverberated through the small box of the room.

His mother grunted and took a slug of Bud. There was never a shortage of brew in the Garko house. "Get me a ciggie, will you?"

Gerald didn't want to reveal his hands, but saying no to his mother was dangerous. Big as she was, when she finally found her feet, she could take a swipe that would K.O. a grizzly bear. He grabbed her pack of Camels and tossed them onto her lap.

She gave him a sour look. "Whatsa matter, boy? You got no manners?"

Gerald shrugged and escaped into the bathroom, closing the thin door. He exhaled slowly, hoping to ease the pounding that felt like he'd swallowed a thunderstorm. When he turned on the light, Gerald avoided the mirror because he hated how he looked: the acne blooming across his coarse skin, the dirty brown hair fringing his forehead, the curly sideburns inching onto his cheeks, and worst of all, his narrow shoulders and chest, which he prayed would fill out like his father's. On most days, he'd as soon take a piss out in the woods than be in this small space, especially one holding him captive with his reflection, but today he had no choice.

Gerald took courage and glanced at himself. The fear staring back at him was shocking. His eyes looked tight, like he'd forgotten how to blink. And then there was the blood. Gerald reached for the bar of Ivory soap and began to scour his hands and shirt, but the oil and blood were stubborn. He took off his shirt, pumped some pink Dab-A-Do hand cleaner from the jug sitting above the toilet, and scrubbed again, finally having success. After folding his shirt over his arm and checking his white T-shirt and black pants for stains, he left the bathroom and headed for the kitchen.

"Gerald? How 'bout a coupla sandwiches for breakfast?" his mother yelled.

He didn't have to ask what kind. It didn't matter what was in the sandwiches, just so they were thick with meat. When he took out some bologna, Kraft's mayo, and a stack of sliced American cheese from the fridge, his hands were shaking. "Jesus Christ," he whispered, as he placed his fingers flat on the cutting board. "What the hell?" But he knew why they were shaking. His entire body still had the weevie-jeevies. In fact, the smell of the bologna made him want to puke. Fresh perspiration popped out on his forehead, and his heart was beating like he'd run a mile. He swiped at the sweat and dealt out six slices of Wonder bread on the counter and slathered each with mayo. When he was finished constructing the sandwiches, he stacked them on a plate and brought them into his mother. Clouds of smoke encircled her head. Gerald breathed it in, trying to feel normal.

"Where's yours?" she asked him.

"Not hungry."

"Go on, then. You're skinny as all get out. Whatsa matter with your appetite?"

It was true he was thin, but the more he watched his mother shove food down her throat, the less he could eat. "I'll catch somethin' later, Ma." He grabbed a dirty shirt from the back of his father's leather chair, slipped it on, then plunked down on the cracked seat and let the TV noise wash over him.

About 10:45, there was a rap on the screen. Gerald's eyes snapped open. His mother looked at him and jutted a chin toward the door. Gerald turned and saw a policeman, Mike Dybek, through the window. He was bareheaded and wearing a blue uniform. Gerald stood on shaky legs and opened the door. Even though Mike was from Stardust Lake, he was still a cop, and no one in Stardust Lake liked cops.

"Hi, Gerald. We got a few questions to ask you."

Gerald didn't like the sound of this. Behind him, his mother leaned forward. He could tell because she grunted from the exertion and the floor creaked. Rather than let his mother hear their conversation, Gerald stepped outside and walked down the cinderblock steps onto the grass.

"Harvey ever goin' get this heap fixed?" the policeman asked, pointing to the Mercury.

Gerald figured this was a good sign, that the cop was being so casual. Feeling braver, he said, "Nah, not likely. You know how it is."

Mike Dybek nodded. There were six old cars clogging driveways in town: a Studebaker, a Ford Fairlane, two Plymouth Barracudas—one being cannibalized for the other—the Garko Merc, and a VW van owned by some druggy-hippie types who'd hightailed it away from the law and run out of real estate here on the U.S. side of Lake Ontario. Several boats were also beached on street corners, their trailers long removed. What died in Stardust Lake usually stayed in Stardust Lake.

"Well, Gerald, I should speak with you in front of one of your parents."

"Ma ain't feelin' too well..."

Mike Dybek nodded, knowing what ailed her. "And your father?"

Gerald shrugged. "Payday was yesterday."

"Okay. I guess I know where Harvey is." He ran a hand over the Mercury's fender, appreciating the metal. "How old are you?"

"Nearly nineteen." He thought for a moment and added, "Still in high school."

"Got left back a few times?"

"Yeah, guess so."

"Well, it's okay then. Not having your parents here." The policeman abruptly stopped walking. "Gerald, we got a call awhile ago."

Gerald glanced at the policeman, trying to steer his eyes away from the man's holster, spit-shined black shoes, shiny gold badge, and bulging chest. "Yeah?"

"Yeah. Seems there was some kind of accident down by Stardust Lake. Last night. Maybe this morning."

Since no question had been asked, Gerald was silent.

"A bad accident," the cop added. "You know anything about it?"

"No."

Mike Dybek ran a big hand over his blond buzz-cut hair. "A woman was hurt real bad."

Gerald remained quiet, though he let a little concern peek through his eyes.

"Yeah, in fact she's dead."

Gerald snuck a quick breath. She'd been alive when he left. Or at least he thought she was. "Who?" he asked, hearing the quiver in his voice.

"You tell me."

"Hell if I know."

The policeman gave him a sharp look. "We think you do."

"Nah. Not me. I been fishin' 'n stuff." He pointed to a black six-foot casting rod.

"Catch anything?"

"Nope."

Mike Dybek was getting annoyed. Gerald could sense this, so he said, "Had me a longnose sucker, but he got clean away." This lie made him feel better. It had the ring of truth to it. In fact, he almost believed he'd been fishing.

"Well, while you were *fishing*, did you happen to run into Hawk McKenny?"

The confidence drained out of Gerald. "Saw him in school yesterday."

The policeman scraped his bottom lip along his upper teeth. "You better be straight with me, boy."

"Yeah. Sure. History class. Last period." To Gerald's ears, it sounded like he was lying his face off.

"I think it was this morning. And you know what? I think we better go to the station. Sweat the story out of you."

That was all Gerald had to hear. He turned and ran. Mike Dybek did, too, but Gerald was faster, even with his awkward gait. He ran across Willow Street, dodging an old saggy yellow mutt drifting across his path, then flew down Oak Lane to Lakeside

Drive, which ran parallel to the beach, made a right and headed for the town limits, which took almost no time to reach since Stardust Lake was a community of nineteen houses. He heard the cop yelling at him to stop and was afraid that Dybek would shoot. This made Gerald sprint full out until he hung a left and came upon the pedestrian bridge. One sign warned: "No Outlet." Another: "Dead End." Well, he thought, they got that right.

As he leapt onto the first steps of the bridge, he caught his toe and went flying forward, thudding into the wood planking. Gerald rose, but Mike Dybek's heavy body slammed on top of him.

"You little white trash bastard!" the policeman grunted, as he threw his arm around Gerald's neck, hauled him to his feet, spun him around, and handcuffed him. Then he looped his arm through Gerald's. "You're gonna wish you never'd done that."

Gerald snuck a glance at the cop's face. It was red like the rare roast beef they served on platters at the Down 'n Easy Diner. His body even smelled like beef—masculine, powerful. "I didn't do nothin'," Gerald mumbled.

As they walked to the police cruiser, men standing by their pick-up trucks, drinking beer and gossiping, stared at Gerald and squinted their eyes at Mike Dybek. The only good thing about living in Stardust Lake was that if you did something wrong, you had plenty of company, Gerald thought. Up to now, he hadn't gotten into too much trouble or rather hadn't been caught.

They pulled to the curb in front of the temporary police station that served four lakeshore communities. Composed of three trailers arranged in an "H," the station didn't look mobile or temporary since each trailer rested on a cement foundation. Mike Dybek pulled him out of the car, pushed him down the path splotched with grass clumps and brown earth, up four metal steps, inside, and then thrust a chair at him. "Sit down," he ordered. "I got to check on things."

Gerald sat and looked around. The place was full of paper: dozens of thumbtacked-notices peeling off bulletin boards and piles of it in manila folders stacked on metal desks. Cigarette smoke and sugared-coffee smells dominated, which made sense since drinking coffee and smoking seemed to be the primary activities except for gawking at him, which everyone was doing: the dispatcher, the secretary, and another cop. Although he was used to disapproving looks, this was worse. He dropped his eyes to the squares of sand-colored linoleum, noticing that someone had spilled coffee that matched the tiles.

Then, a second later, his mother stomped in, grunting and wheezing, as she turned sidewise through the front door. She was wearing a gray hooded sweatshirt and green sweatpants. Her mouth, painted in red lipstick, was clenched around a cigarette, her eyes nearly closed from the onslaught of smoke. When she saw Gerald, she stopped.

"What's my boy done!" she shouted to the dispatcher. It was not a question.

Hearing her, Dybek poked his head in the room. "You ask him, Hilda."

"He under arrest?"

Dybek glared at her. "We'll deal with you in a moment. Gerald, you sit there and don't get any ideas about leaving."

Gerald slumped low in the chair. Dybek returned to the second trailer.

Hilda Garko parked herself on a bench a few feet from Gerald. "Christ, you dumb fool!" she whispered in a loud voice. "Don't you know better than to get mixed up with this bunch?"

Gerald looked at his mother and felt miserable. "How'd you get here?"

"I called Duff. He brought me in the pick-up. But how I got here ain't no never mind, Gerald. You answer your mother."

"I stole a bike, that's all." He stared at his sneakers.

"Sweet Jesus! How many times I tell you to stay clear of the law? How many times? Specially that bastard Chief Kruegger. You don't wanna mess with him. He's crazy mean." Hilda Garko frowned deep furrows in her forehead and leaned toward Gerald. "Now you keep your trap shut and don't tell Harvey least wise we both suffer…but once long ago when I was fourteen and a pretty young thing, Kruegger hurt me bad. Told me if I ever squealed…well," she took a drag on her cigarette, "…I didn't. So you listen to me. That's why I can't stick around here. Just can't. I come to see where you were. When Harvey gets in, I'll send him over…if he can stand up. Meanwhile you keep quiet and don't give 'em any 'scuse to get mad, hear?" She came to her feet and narrowed her eyes at Gerald. "Are you sure that's all you done? Steal a bike?"

"That's all, Ma. There's some other business they think I got mixed up in, but I didn't."

"Well, okay, then. You watch out, Gerald."

After his mother left, Gerald wished he'd told her the whole story, wished that she'd stay with him. He laid his head in his hands and waited until Dybek returned. When he did, Police Chief Herm Kruegger was behind him. Gerald stared at Kruegger's cold blue eyes and started to sweat rivers.

"Hey, Mike. What do we have here?" the police chief asked.

"This here is Gerald Garko," Dybek said.

Kruegger's mouth hitched up under his blond mustache, and he said with obvious disgust, "Yeah, I know the Garkos. Fill me in on what's going on."

Mike Dybek took Kruegger by the arm and they stepped away. Gerald only caught a few phrases—something about bicycle tracks, narrow ones, by the lake. He knew it wouldn't be long before the police uncovered the hidden road bike. And when they did, he would be in even more hot water. Then he heard the girl's name: Doris Mondello, a local prostitute who was passed between the biker guys, the truckers, and the construction boys. Gerald knew his dad had bopped her a few times, or so he had bragged one night when he was drunk and horny and pissed because he never got any from Gerald's mother.

"Hey, I didn't do nothing…honest!" Gerald cried, but the two policemen ignored him, so he sat on the uncomfortable chair and stewed, visualizing Doris Mondello lying naked in the water, her torn clothes thrown by the lake's edge. When he shut his eyes, he saw the pretty reflections of the colored leaves in the water, but then there was a lot of red blood there, too. He didn't want to think about that.

After a secretary passed Kruegger a note, he went outside and returned twenty minutes later with the Merlin bike, which he lifted by the handlebars and set against the wall. "Geez," he said to Dybek, "Forgot the damned gloves. Well, no problem. My fingerprints are on record." He pulled out a handkerchief, spat on his hands, and wiped them clean. Then he came over to Gerald. "So, we found your new bike, Gerald. Nice. Real nice. Blood on the handlebars. Did you know that?"

The steely glint in the cop's eyes reminded Gerald of sun striking the chrome of the Merc. He stared at the man's thick neck, where the blue collar bit into flesh, and shrugged.

"Ah, cut the crap, will you?" the chief said. "Where'd you get the bike?"

"I found it."

Mike Dybek's massive body blocked the small amount of light squeezing through the window. "Where?"

"Don't recall. Maybe by the lake or somewheres." Gerald's brain was spinning faster than a merry-go-round.

Dybek did a bad mimic of Gerald's voice. "*I found it by the lake.* Well, Christ, we *know* that! That's because a witness saw you with it and got suspicious. Then the guy walked to the lake and saw the body. Called us right after."

Kruegger lowered his voice to a growl. "What time were you over there? What did you see?"

Sweat was slipping down Gerald's face. "'Round nine o'clock. And I ain't seen nothin' at all. I just took the bike. I'm sorry I stole it."

"You're lying, Gerald," said Dybek. "Where did the blood come from?"

"Fishin'..."

Kruegger shook his head in exasperation and said to Dybek, "Not only is this kid guilty, but he's stupid. Take off the cuffs, Mike. Let's see where this boy cut himself."

Dybek followed orders and then rolled up Gerald's sleeves.

"So where're you hurt, huh?" Kruegger stared at Gerald, who didn't answer. "Well, Mike, guess we got ourselves the murderer."

"Looks like," Dybek agreed.

"No! It wasn't me!" Gerald cried. "It was Hawk…Hawk McKenny. He did it."

"Yeah, right…it's always the Indian," Dybek retorted.

"It was!"

"Let's go and get this on tape," Kruegger said.

The policemen lifted Gerald out of the chair and brought him into the second trailer, where he was placed at a desk in front of a microphone. Kruegger sat in the chair opposite, dictated the particulars, and read the Miranda rights. When the cop gave the nod, Gerald explained how he'd been walking in the woods above the lake and had seen Hawk next to Doris Mondello.

"He was…well, you know…" Gerald wasn't actually sure what he'd seen, the more he went over the scene in his mind.

"Raping her?" Dybek suggested, circling behind Gerald.

"Yeah!" Gerald was relieved to have an answer. Anything to get these guys to leave him alone. "He musta ripped off her clothes and hit her with a rock or somethin' 'cause she was a mess. Bleedin' and all."

"You're telling us the God's honest truth?" Kruegger asked.

"Yeah. That's what I seen. And when he'd done…you know…with what he was doing…Hawk, he rolled her into the water."

"I see," said Mike Dybek. "So how'd you get blood on your hands? One of our boys found your wet shirt at your house. You missed a few spots."

Shit, Gerald thought. "Well, I guess I went down to see if she was okay."

"You guess?" Dybek stood to Gerald's left.

Gerald nodded. "She weren't dead or nothin'. Not so's I could tell."

Dybek shook his head. "So you left her there to die, right? And then took the bike?"

"She wasn't goin' use it no more!"

The two policemen exchanged angry glances. "Well," Kruegger began, "your pal Hawk tells a different story."

"Huh?"

"Yeah, he says he found the victim by the lake and saw you hanging around."

"Oh, no!" Gerald bolted to his feet. "I ain't done it!"

Dybek laid a heavy hand on his shoulder, pressing Gerald into the chair. "Yeah, you did. Maybe you wanted some free pussy, boy, or maybe you wanted that fancy bicycle, but either way, you did it."

There was a knock on the door and another policeman entered the room. He gestured for Dybek and Kruegger to join him in the corner. A few minutes later, after some conversation, the man left, and Kruegger returned to his chair.

"So, this bicycle. Doris Mondello didn't own one, and besides, it's a man's bike. Is it Hawk McKenny's?" the chief asked.

"Don't think so."

"I doubt that it is," Mike Dybek said to Kruegger. "Too expensive. Not unless the kid stole it from somewhere else."

"He don't have no bike," Gerald repeated.

"So if it isn't his and it isn't yours, whose is it?" Dybek asked.

"Don't know."

Dybek glanced at Kruegger. "Maybe there was someone else there. One of Doris' clients."

The two men stared at each other, turned off the tape recorder, and exited the room. Gerald heard the door's lock click.

What the hell was going on? Did they believe him about Hawk? But then they said he had killed Doris and that the bicycle was someone else's. Jesus Christ he was confused, whirling with feeling guilty and not feeling guilty, worrying what Hawk would do to him. He was scared shitless about that, thinking of the hunting knife Hawk carried in his boot, and then Dad, oh, my God! His father would come home plastered and find out what was going on and would hit the roof. Gerald didn't know who to be frightened of the most. Kruegger and Dybek? Getting the electric chair? Tears began to slip out of his eyes. He felt like a trapped muskrat he'd seen once in the woods, its teeth working at its leg, trying to bite it off so he could get free. Everyone had their jaws on him. Dad would whop him good, maybe even kill him. And besides what his mother had told him, he'd heard tales about Kruegger beating some kid to death just because he sassed him.

Gerald's mouth was dry. The tan walls seemed suddenly closer, tightening around him, inch by inch. He felt sick again. Dizzy. He saw Doris and all that blood. Hawk turning to look at him hard, hating him like his worst enemy rather than his best friend. If he thought he'd ratted on him, Gerald knew what Hawk would do.

He jumped up and ran around the rectangular circumference of the enclosure, bumping into the table like he was blind. The pain to his shin reverberated to his brain, dazzling him with its tiny electricity and edging him into crazy panic.

"Let me out!" he wailed, "Please!"

No one came.

He trotted halfway around the room and shoved the table, creating a space so he could get by. Then he began to lope in slow circles, trying to dispel the fear, pressing his elbow against the walls as a guide, as if doing so would force them backward. With each revolution, he told himself he'd be okay, that this was just a bad dream like the nightmares he'd had as a little boy. Of course those weren't really nightmares. His Dad really had done those things. Those bad things like they were accusing him of doing. Messing with him when he was a kid, nearly killing his older brother in a knife fight. Somehow, his father always got away with everything. Gerald wished he could, too, though all he'd done was take a bicycle.

Gerald lowered his head, wanting to block the sight of the walls closing in, and kept running, terrified to stop despite his ragged breathing and the pressure building in his ears.

"Help! Please! I didn't do it!" he yelled.

After more turns around the room, his lungs ran out of air and he collapsed on the table. Sweat and tears ran down his face. His shirt was soaked.

"Where the hell is he?"

It was his father's voice, coming from the center trailer. Dybek and Kruegger were yelling, a woman screamed, and suddenly the lock clicked, the door flew open, and his father crashed in. Gerald straightened up and backed quickly against the wall.

"You stupid little bastard!" His father shouted. The sweet smell of alcohol and the acrid stench of smoke swirled in the room as his father stepped toward him, fists clenched, his shoulder-length hair streaked across his angry face. "What did you do, Gerald? You useless shit!"

The two policemen grabbed Harvey Garko's arms, but Harvey wasn't in a docile mood. He twisted away and ran at Gerald, throwing a punch that knocked him flat to the floor. Gerald raised his hands to protect himself and stared up at his father's ripped red-plaid flannel shirt, black Pittsburgh Steelers' baseball cap, and stained blue jeans. But mostly he saw his eyes—dark with fury. He knew those eyes too well.

Dybek tried to wrap his arms around Harvey's bull chest, but as strong as the policeman was, he was no match for a drunk's rage.

"Get off me, you fuckin' pig!" Harvey screamed as he shoved Dybek away, lost his balance, and fell to his knees.

Kruegger sprang forward and grabbed Harvey's shirt, hauling him upright. As Dybek came from behind, the two men tried to force Harvey flat against the table, but Harvey got his legs under him and blasted into Dybek, knocking him over. As Gerald crawled into the corner of the room, his father set upon him and delivered a vicious kick.

"You no-good son of a bitch!" Harvey yelled, slamming a black engineer boot into Gerald's side.

Gerald felt a stab of pain. His father kicked him in the thigh, and was about to strike again, but Gerald rolled to his right.

As his father charged after him, a third cop entered and all three policemen tried to subdue his father, who was finally tackled by Kruegger. The police chief began throwing punches, sharp and professional, like a boxer. Though Gerald was the lightweight of the group and was as frightened of his father as the cops, he forced himself to his feet and head-butted Kruegger in the shoulder. The two of them smashed into the chair and table. Dazed and hurt, Gerald untangled himself from blue-uniformed arms and legs and found his feet. The third cop was helping Dybek bash his father so Gerald ran for the door, plowing through the dispatcher and secretary, who were watching the chaos in the interrogation room. As he was about to rush outside, he saw Hawk McKenny sitting in the third trailer, fumbling with a ring of keys, trying to unlock the handcuffs on his wrists.

Hawk looked up and saw him. "What the shit is goin' on?" His black hair, usually combed straight to his shoulder, was a mess and he had a red welt on his cheek.

Gerald hesitated, trying to read the expression on Hawk's face but couldn't. "Let's get outta here." He sprinted through the door with Hawk a step behind him.

"Where're we goin' to?" Hawk asked, as they circled around the police station.

Gerald's ribs were aching, but he could still breathe, so his lungs were okay. Probably nothing was broken. "Woods," he replied.

The two took off, stopping once in Larry Wreblewski's yard.

"He's the one snitched on me," Gerald told Hawk.

"Bastard!"

"Yeah." Even though it hurt, Gerald picked up a brick and hurled it through the bay window of the Wreblewski's house. When they heard shouts, he yelled, "Hey, he's got a shotgun. Come on."

Gerald sprinted away with Hawk following. They hurried through a meadow, fighting pricker bushes and poison ivy. Ten minutes later, avoiding most of the town, they crossed Lakeshore Drive and slipped into the forest surrounding Stardust Lake.

"Look at the police tape," Gerald pointed out, as they approached the water.

"Just like on TV."

"Yeah. Don't think we better hang around here. Cops might be back."

Hawk nodded and leaned against a tree. "Lemme rest for a minute, okay?"

"Yeah, sure." Gerald kneeled on the ground.

"Hey, can you try these keys?" Hawk asked.

Gerald stared at him. Was it safe to uncuff Hawk, who had accused him of murdering Doris or, worse yet, might think he'd finked on him to the cops? Still, he and Hawk were buddies and in a fix. He took the ring of keys from Hawk and inserted each key, but none worked.

Hawk shrugged. "Just my fuckin' luck."

"Sorry." Gerald looked at his friend. "So, what happened this mornin'?"

Hawk's black eyes narrowed. "I seen you and you seen me."

"I know that. But—"

"I came on Doris lying there, near dead. Just was lookin', you know, to be sure."

"Well, I didn't do it," Gerald said. "No way, man."

"So that explains it." Hawk sat on his haunches. "Larry Wreblewski never seen me, but the cops picked me up anyway." He swiped at the sweat rolling down his face. "Shit. If you didn't do it and I didn't do it, then I know who did and it ain't good for us."

"Oh?"

"Yeah. You know who I seen with the bike?"

"Who?"

Hawk chewed his thumb. "Well, it's like this. I'm headin' to the lake to go fishin' for sunnies, and I seen this guy real upset at this here bike. Seems the tire's gone flat so he can't ride it. When he hears me comin', he spooks and runs away. Even when he seen it's only me, he don't stop. Then I get to wondering and go down to the lake. That's when I seen Doris bloody and naked. Next thing I know, you come along and act all weird and everythin'. You grab the bike like it's yours and scram like you was guilty. Hell, I didn't think that bike was yours, but I figured you mighta stole it and left it there when you did the dirt on Doris." He sighed. "Christ, Gerald! We're fuckin' screwed!"

Gerald tried to piece together all the parts he knew with what Hawk was telling him. "So you seen the guy who done it. Who was it, man?"

Hawk shook his head. "I ain't no snitch!"

Gerald grabbed Hawk's arm. "This ain't no time for that! You gotta tell me 'cause whoever it is might come back. You know, like they do. Scene of the crime and all." He looked around the dense woods and felt a chill creep up his spine.

"*He* done it."

Gerald's head hurt from his father's punch and all the confusion. "Who?"

Just then, leaves rustled. Herm Kruegger walked through the trees with a small black gun aimed at them. Gerald noticed that Kruegger's police .38 was parked in its holster and that the police chief was wearing latex gloves.

Hawk took one look at Kruegger and ran. Without hesitation, Kruegger fired. Hawk pitched forward onto the ground, red spreading across the back of his white shirt.

Kruegger turned toward Gerald. "They always return to the scene of the crime." He gave Gerald a strange smile.

Gerald stared at Hawk and swallowed hard. Suddenly he knew who the "he" was. "Yeah. Guess they do."

Kruegger's eyes frosted with anger. "Lie down and don't move."

Gerald did as he was ordered. Kruegger removed four live bullets from the gun's chamber and pocketed them. "You know, it's just a matter of respect. If that stupid whore hadn't fussed about giving me a freebie, I'd probably be arresting you for peeing in the road or something." He lifted Gerald off the ground and walked him to within a few feet of Hawk's motionless body. "One bullet left." He drew his .38 and inserted the tip into Gerald's left ear and then forced the smaller gun into Gerald's right hand, encircling his own hand tightly around Gerald's and aiming at Hawk's head. "Pull the trigger," he instructed, removing his hand.

"No!" Gerald's legs went weak.

"Do it or you're dead."

Hawk wasn't breathing. His friend had gone to *Aronhia*, the heaven Hawk's Huron mother believed in. One more bullet wouldn't make a difference. Gerald held his breath, fired, and instantly closed his eyes. The sound skimmed across the flat of the lake and disappeared in the trees.

Kruegger took the gun from Gerald and tossed it into the bushes. "Prints, powder residue, and a white trash kid who killed Doris Mondello and his friend who witnessed everything." The police chief chuckled as he holstered the .38. "Pretty damned neat. And I even get to be the arresting officer." He reached behind him for handcuffs.

Gerald remembered the panic he felt in the interrogation room. That's the way he would feel in prison, only the room would be much smaller. And then there was the possibility of the electric chair.

"No!" he screamed, as his fist landed on Kruegger's chin.

The policeman reeled and dropped the handcuffs. Gerald smashed a left against the man's cheek, turned, and ran toward the thickest part of the forest. As he scrambled up an eroded bank and grabbed a white birch tree, a shot rang out, then another. Gerald felt the impact in his leg and back. He kept going, though everything was slowing down until finally he wasn't moving at all. He looked up and saw yellow birch leaves fluttering against a dark gray sky. It would rain soon, he thought. He could smell the sweet dampness in the air.

The third bullet knocked him to earth.

When Herm Kruegger flipped him over, Gerald couldn't see anything—not the cop's face or the yellow leaves or the stormy sky.

"I ain't done nothin'," he whispered.

The cop grunted. "Yeah, you stupid son of a bitch, and you never will."

Words Leave Me Hungry

By Allison Whittenberg

What do cannibals do about dinner
when there is nobody around?
I remember the first time I had sex only because
every other time was better.
Do all journeys last forever?
I don't write much any more
just a line or two
per year
If the past is deep,
is the future shallow?
They don't come,
the visions
All I see is nothing
And more nothing
It's not like when I was young and throbbing
neath that body so much larger than mine
everything was bigger than me back then
bigger, bolder
There is no substitute for human contact
Words leave me hungry.

The Quickening

By Allison Whittenberg

Because I believe in perfection
I believe in abortion
Babies are asymmetrical
They/she/he/it squander
The silken grammar of routine
But, a fetus can be edited
Its absence assures a lacy indefectibility
In the vacuum, I can breathe
It's not right
It's not the right time
I don't want to hunker down in Staten Island
Or be on bed rest
Or buy big clothes
Or rush to alter with a gown and a groom and a promise
With rice raining on me
          like fallout.
I don't want to be folk like my mother was folk.
Children growing out of her hairdo.
Dull eyes and unpainted nails.
Waking on the hour to feed. Feeding. Always feeding the hungry.
The weeping.
Little ones pursuing happiness.
Little ones rob happiness.
Fuzzy fussy responsibilities piling like landfills
On and on and on, like a heartbeat.
I believe in change and wants and modernity and choice.

Lights Out

By Gretchen Cruz

Carla turned around anxiously when she heard the metal doors opening behind her. It was not the fact that they had opened that scared her. No. In fact, she took pleasure in the moments where she could walk out of her cell, even if confinement followed her everywhere she went. The white of her room was overwhelming. It made her think of the world outside, of the brightness of the sun; it made everything seem so much darker.

"Come on Mrs. Jenner. I won't stand here all day. You coming out or not?" said the guard. Officer Fillmore. Now this guard, this guard was the one who made her shake. He was built, tall, had that arrogant air about him. He reminded her of Paul. Her precious Paul, her ghost Paul. No. She could not go down that road again. It was too much to bear.

"Yes I'm coming Mr. Fillmore. Would not miss recreation for the world." She attempted a smile, but it went unnoticed. She was already being shackled for exercise. It might not have been the most efficient was to exercise, but it was the only way. Having no options, no control, was something she was used to. Her prison had begun decades ago. Three years in solitary confinement was just an expansion of this prison. And it would all end at some point. She was looking forward to it. Death was welcome. Death was imminent. And there was no going back.

****

The first time Dr. Wesley came was the night she woke up screaming from a nightmare. She had those often. They were usually of Paul, but this time, they were also of Jenny.

Every night after that Dr. Wesley came for a visit in her cell. That was what he would call them, visits for the solitary. She knew better. He was a counselor, he was appointed to her because everyone thought she was crazy. That she was a threat to herself, just like she was a threat to everyone around her. Well maybe she was. But the reality of it was that nobody had ever cared enough to get her help. So if prison came with a personal counselor, then so be it. All the better.

"How is the cell treating you Carla?" he would say every time to start up conversation. The best part about it was that he would always use her first name. Nobody around here seemed to do that. It was always Mrs. Jenner. But that was not really her last name; it never had been.

"Everything is always the same Dr. Wesley. It is hot, and the bed is a bit uncomfortable, but it is all a matter of getting used to. I don't think you could make me sleep in a comfortable bed if you tried to now!" Humor was truly the only thing that kept her going at this point.

"What nightmare have you woken to this time that I have been summoned so late in the evening?" he said. "I do have a family you know."

"Yeah, your daughter must be mad at you. Always coming off to see me in the middle of the night."

"Well, it is all a part of the job you know. She truly loves me, and she knows that I love her more than anything in the world, so it doesn't matter. It is my wife that gets mad." His eyes would light up every time he talked about his daughter.

"Yeah, I guess. My mom would always get mad when my dad left the room in the middle of the night."

"Your dad? We haven't really talked about him. What was he like?" he said.

"You remind me a lot of him Dr. Wesley, except that you remind me of all the things he was that you are not. Does that make sense?" Carla shuddered. Dr. Wesley was all the things she had wanted in her father, which only made her think of all the things her father was.

"No Carla, can you elaborate a little further?" These were the occasions when Dr. Wesley would take out his pad and pen. He said he was writing things down so that he would not forget. Carla was important to him, he would say. And everything she said to him was of utmost importance. He cared about her, and she always felt like she could trust him with her deepest secrets.

"As I said, Father would also leave my mom's bed in the middle of the night. Just like you." Carla said, her eyes scrunched and distant, as if digging in the deepest recesses of her mind. As if all she was about to divulge had been hidden to the world for a long time.

"And where would he go Carla?" His voice was soothing.

"He said he loved me too much to sleep without me. That I kept the monsters at bay." Carla was now holding her own hands, clenching and unclenching her fists.

"And how did that make you feel Carla?" He was writing furiously by this point, without ever taking his eyes off her. She looked too vulnerable for him to ignore.

"Well, I guess I was confused. Fathers should not fear monsters. And there were still my own monsters to deal with."

"Your own monsters?" he asked.

"I loved him very much, I was supposed to right? He was my father. But then, something changed. He changed. He let go of his monsters. And he used me to do so." By this time, Carla was slightly shaking.

"What do you mean? What monsters are you talking about?" He stopped writing and paid close attention; he had a feeling that whatever was about to unfold was going to be crucial.

"He had a disease, he would say. And then he would apologize to me, and said he could not help it. It was just what he liked. But he said that he still loved me more than anything."

"What did he like Carla?" The room was silent. All you could hear was the distinct, and slightly unnerving sound of the overhead lights beaming. It took her three minutes to answer.

"…Little girls, little girls like me." Dr. Wesley stared at her. A sole tear ran down her face. She was in another world though. He needed to get her back to the surface, to realize just what she had admitted to.

"Is that why you killed him?" Carla's face snapped back to Dr. Wesley's. His comment had the desired effect.

"I didn't kill him. He died of an overdose. It was accidental. He gave himself too much insulin. The coroner said so." Her voice was shaking and she seemed very nervous and frantic. It was as if she was trying to convince herself.

"Carla, you and I both know that that is not true. Your father was a doctor. He knew exactly how much insulin he could take. You were there, you picked him up from work that day because your mom was out of town that day. You were sixteen and you knew how much insulin was too much. He had shown you and your mom in any case of emergency. You went to his bedroom that night, just like he would crawl into your bedroom when you were just six. He had taken his sleep medication, so he didn't realize you had nicked him. You gave him the extra insulin. You watched him while he died. You constantly checked his pulse and when he was gone, you called 911. You were just lucky you were not caught. He didn't expect it."

Dr. Wesley's voice had been gradually rising. Carla had taken to covering her ears. She was now sobbing uncontrollably. She finally burst.

"It was not my fault! It was not my fault! He did this, he turned me into this monster!" She felt relieved after these words. Someone knew. And it was Dr. Wesley. He would understand, he always did.

"That's right. You were the victim here. You have always been the victim. Everything is going to be okay Carla. It will all end soon. You can go back to sleep now. Sweet dreams." She closed her eyes, and when she reopened them he was already gone.

****

The noise was bothering her again. She was still getting used to the quiet. In the four years she had been in this place, she had yet to get used to the soundless noise that confined her. The silence was too loud, the walls too thick, the air too congested. Everything was caving in, but she had no way of climbing out. Her thoughts were becoming all too consuming. Her deafening mind starkly contrasted to the stillness around her.

"I want to talk about your husband, Carla. Describe him to me." Dr. Wesley was perched in his usual chair, his demeanor ragged.

"You look tired Dr. Wesley." Carla had seen his weariness setting in.

Over the past few months, he had become less energetic. It was as if the life drained out of him the more she opened up to him.

"I am tired Carla. So tired."

"Is it me? Are you going to stop coming to our visits?" Her vulnerability reminded him of a child, so innocent, so broken.

"No Carla. I will always be here as long as you need me to be. You are in control, remember? Now tell me, how did Paul treat you?" Carla looked away as soon as his name was spoken. She could not bear to think of him sometimes. Her precious Paul.

"He was tall, built, handsome. I met him through my mother you know. She set us up after Father...well you know...." She looked back at Dr. Wesley who just nodded in understanding.

"Anyways, he was charming. So charming. I remember the first time I met him I fell in love. He seemed so caring, like a provider you know. He would be the man that would protect me."

"Whom did you need protection from?" Dr. Wesley was back to writing in his pad.

"I don't know. But everyone was always talking about how important it was to marry someone strong. To protect you."

"Well did he live up to that? Did he protect you?" Dr. Wesley looked at her expectantly.

"At first. He would be so nice to me you know. He really loved me. And then we had Jenny..." Carla looked at him then and smiled.

"I wish you could have met her. She was quite the little girl." Carla's smile diminished now. It was as if her thin frame could not bear the weight of a smile.

"Paul really loved her you know. Just like he loved me. But he said he just needed more. His space and his freedom. So he would take off at night. You men can never stay with your wives all night can you?" Carla was now accusatory. She had spent her time in prison remembering the perfection of Paul; a perfection that was rather contradicted by the appalling truth.

"Maybe he just needed his space like you mentioned. Maybe all he did was drive around at night." Carla laughed wildly at this. She sounded maniacal.

"I don't think so Dr. Wesley. You see, I believed that at first. I believed it fervently. So I decided to dig in. Get the facts straight." Carla paused for some seconds. It was as if she was trying tc piece the story together.

"I followed him one night. I climbed out of bed, and I got my car keys when I heard the garage open. I followed him all night."

"And where did he go Carla?" Carla snapped her head back to me with a look of dread on her face.

"Nowhere. He went nowhere. He just drove around all night." Dr. Wesley took off his wire-rimmed glasses. His hands went to his face in frustration.

"Carla, I need you to explain why you strangled Paul! Why did you drown Jenny? If Paul was just going out for a drive, why did you hate him so much?" She felt his frustration through his voice.

"I didn't kill Jenny." Carla had stood up dramatically and was now pacing the tiny room. The walls were caving in on her again.

"Yes you did Carla. Stop kidding yourself. You were found cradling her body in the bathtub. The coroner established that Paul had been dead before her, which makes it impossible for Paul to have done it. Just admit it to yourself! Why did you do it? Why Jenny?"

"She was dead long before then!" Carla screeched. She was breathing deeply, as if she could not get enough air into her lungs.

"All I did was save her from a life of torment. Don't you see? She never really had a chance. None of us women do. Men take advantage of us, just like my father took advantage of me…Paul would have done her wrong eventually. It started out with the outings at night. Then when I confronted him, he screamed at me and called me crazy. Crazy? Me?" she huffed.

"Then, it all changed. He started taking Jenny with him; he said that I was behaving erratically. He said he was going to his Mom's and taking Jenny with him." All of a sudden, Carla got on her knees and held Dr. Wesley's gaze. He had to understand why she did what she did. It was as if he was pleading for mercy.

"You have to understand Dr. Wesley. He was going to take her away from me. I think Paul loved Jenny too much if you know what I mean. So I did the best thing I could for them. I ended it, plain and simple. He had to stop doing what he was doing. And I didn't want her to end up like me."

Tears were streaming down her face.

"Like you?" Dr. Wesley asked.

"Paranoid. I don't trust anyone you see. You are the only person I trust Dr. Wesley."

"Did it ever occur to you that not all men are the same? That Paul was never taking advantage of Jenny? That you made it all up in your mind?" Carla was shaking her head emphatically, her round eyes huge in fear.

"No Dr. Wesley. They are all the same! They are all the same! They are all the same. They are all the same." Carla was crouched on the floor, holding her head and moving back and forth.

"Quiet in there, Mrs. Jenner!" Officer Fillmore banged on the steel door.

"What's wrong with her?" Officer Modarres was new in the unit. He had still not had too much experience with death row inmates. Officer Fillmore was more than happy to warn him.

"She is one of the crazy ones in here. She constantly talks to herself. It mostly happens at nights though when she wakes up screaming from some type of nightmare. Calls out to a Dr. Wesley."

"Dr. Wesley? Is he a counselor here or something?" Modarres had never heard that name.

"Nope. But I did some digging, and talked to the counselor here, apparently Mrs. Jenner was creative enough to just rearrange the letters of his father's last name. He was Dr. Leswey." He shook his head.

"Why would she do that?" Modarres still didn't get it.

"Look Modarres, if you are going to be successful here you are going to have to understand something here. All of the people in here, they had some sort of reason, some sort of motive or drive. They committed their crimes because they rationalized that it was the right thing to do. Now, that doesn't make it right obviously. But it is about trying to decipher why they did what they did." Modarres looked on. Sure, there were reasons, but none of the people here deserved any type of sympathy from him. They were murderers. The worst of the worst at that. He didn't want to start thinking of them as feeling humans, because they were not humans. They were lost souls. They all belonged here.

"Now look at Mrs. Jenner for example. She was abused as a child apparently, from what I can hear from the "conversations" she had with the elusive "Dr. Wesley"." He had taken to using his fingers to quote and unquote parts of his sentence.

"She became some kind of crazy." He continued. "Apparently killed her father, which nobody convicted her for, since she was just sixteen at the time. Nobody knew of the inappropriate behaviors between her and her dad, and nobody could really believe that she would have done such a thing. She went on to get married, had a child, and one day she just went crazy. Strangled the husband, drowned her six-year old daughter, and waited for someone to come into the house and find her."

"Now don't get me wrong. It is all fucked up. But in a way, who can blame her? She is mentally not with it. The counselor here says that she hallucinates this Dr. Wesley as the exact opposite of her father. He makes sense of her crime, so that she does not have to feel the guilt from it."

Fillmore had said it so matter-of-fact, it was hard for Modarres to understand the banal quality that Fillmore had given the situation.

"Okay. So why is she here then? Why not put her in a mental institution?" Fillmore laughed so intensely that Modarres thought that maybe Fillmore had been in this prison too long,

"A mental institution? Please. You lose all your rights once you commit murder, especially if one of the murders involves a six-year old. Nobody cares about the murderers. Nobody cares if they are mentally ill or not. They just want them taken out. Out of society, out of the world. Especially in places where it is okay to have the death penalty. It makes it all that much easier to send someone to their death. Although, if you ask me, some of the people here welcome it. Their entire lives have been a living hell, and death row is not a walk in the park. If you are not crazy when you come in here, you turn crazy throughout your stay. Some of the folks here don't know the difference between reality and fantasy. In a way, ignoring reality and living in your own world is the only escape from death row. That, and death itself of course."

Fillmore kept walking, and left Modarres in front of Mrs. Jenner's cell. The curious man that he was, Modarres looked through the small window in the steel door and stared at Mrs. Jenner. She was reaching out to someone, but she was alone in the room. What a sad case, he thought, but was sure that his opinions about the inmates would not change. They were murderers after all.

****

Officer Modarres went into the small room and sat down with shaking hands. He had been in here before, but never for this purpose, to be a familiar face. He looked around at the faces of all the strangers in the room, and could not fathom why this act was something to be viewed by others. He felt like he was back in time, in Rome, waiting to watch gladiators fight to the death. Cheering them on even.

She was laying down on the bed, hooked up to IVs, and all types of machines surrounded her. Her eyes were closed, her expression relaxed. She was waiting patiently for it all. Modarres knew her well; he had come to know her more than all the other prisoners in the past years.

"Alright, we are ready to get started." The warden had already given the signal that all of this nonsense was about to start. That they were all in for a show, and that everyone but one was going to come out alive. Maybe Modarres would have been the last one to show contempt for such a system some years back. But not now; not after what he had seen. Not after meeting the people he had met. In his past eyes, they should have been monsters, violent. In reality, they were pathetic representations of what they had been. They were already dead.

"Any last words Mrs. Jenner?" Carla opened her eyes then. She looked around the room and her eyes met Modarres. After what seemed like hours, she closed her eyes again and said nothing. What was there to say? The chemicals started flowing. Her breath started becoming shallower and shallower. And then that was it, her last gasp of air. Inconsequential after so many years of long, drawn out appeals. It was over. And so Modarres whispered the only words left to utter.

"Lights out."

Prison Murder, Up Close and Savage: A Collage of Commentaries on *Miller's Revenge*

Miller's Revenge
A novel by Robert Johnson
Brown Paper Publishing, 2010 (137 pages)

Revenge Hurts

By Tim Gallivan

The Real Deal

By Charles Huckelbury

A review and commentary

By Kerry Myers

Revenge Hurts:
A Review of *Miller's Revenge*

By Tim Gallivan

Miller's Revenge, a novel written by Robert Johnson, transports the reader into a sordid place—an American prison. In a narrative describing one long day marked by lethal violence and other atavisms, the reader confronts a few of the sickening realities that are fixtures in the lives of many prisoners. The protagonist, Detective Robert Miller, is employed in an archetypal penal facility, a place in which murder, rape, and suicidal behavior are looming possibilities on any given day. While "Planet Prison" may seem completely alien to anyone who has never visited, this brutal world quickly becomes the norm for those incarcerated or employed within its confines.

From the onset of *Miller's Revenge*, it is apparent that fear is the driving emotion in the prison. Absolutely no one is safe, and one has the sense that there are only two options for the prison's inmates: dominate or be dominated. The Corrections Officers (COs), who are ostensibly charged with maintaining order, often fail to stop the violence they witness. In one of the novel's most gripping scenes, nearby COs fail to act while a young inmate is stabbed and strangled to death on a prison bus. The COs' inaction reinforces the profound instability and pervasive fear of the prison environment.

Certainly, prisoners can try to escape the hell that is prison by seeking the comforts of routine. Miller describes how most life sentence prisoners, colloquially called lifers, want nothing more than to avoid violence and danger and strive to live "in the moment." Many lifers, we learn, establish elaborate and detailed routines so that they can ignore the harsh realities of their environment and achieve some semblance of accomplishment on a daily basis. If all prisoners adopted this mentality, then prison violence would be a rarity. There are, however, "outlaws" in prison: those who want to steal the relative peace and comfort that some prisoners have simply because they are filled with hate and anger. It is these individuals who make prison a jungle.

For this reason, it seems that no one can be unscathed by violence and pain while incarcerated. Knowing this, it becomes rather difficult to judge an inmate's crimes because it is often impossible to determine whether he or she was acting defensively. Even if the conditions do not seem to lend themselves to a clear-cut case of defense, one must always consider the effects that a generally violent atmosphere have on an individual. In response to the constant dangers of the prison environment, an individual might (understandably) become paranoid and excessively defensive.

Hence, Daunte McFadden's murder of Jamal Jordan cannot easily be condemned as cold-blooded homicide because it took place in the unique prison environment. It is certainly arguable that McFadden believed he was in mortal danger because he was called to the gym when it was not his day to attend a basketball game. While most individuals in the free world would not make such a leap, the environment that exists within the incarcerated world makes such leaps necessary for survival.

Although McFadden acknowledged that his information may not have been completely accurate (and Jordan did not actually intend to kill him), he believed that he would die if he did not respond to his perceived threat. As McFadden understood the situation, "If the word is out that I'm a target, then I am a target. Either the word is true and serious bodily harm is set on my ass. Or the word is false but if I don't act — take somebody down — people think I'm lame. Then some other motherfucka will take me down 'cause he think I'm an easy score." When Miller asks McFadden why he could not just walk away, McFadden replies that he had nowhere to go; in prison, there is no refuge from violence.

Even John J. Gibb's (or "Jake the Snake's") behavior presents complexities, making the point that in prison, violence "ain't no clean thing." Things simply aren't black and white. Gibb was a tortured soul, caught in the unrelenting grips of unrequited love. Presumably, this would be an extremely painful ordeal in prison, where love is a scarce commodity that few have the privilege of feeling. Moreover, for Gibb, love was a passionate, all-consuming sentiment that seemed to strip him of his sanity.

By the novel's end, Miller's view of things has unfortunately become jaded. He comes to relish the prospect of putting violent prisoners in the arcane "hole" that lingers on as a relic of cruelty in the prison's dungeon, somehow unsatisfied with the standard brutal option of placing prisoners in solitary confinement. The thought of prisoners suffering greatly in the hole is genuinely gratifying to Miller, whose humane sentiments, clear at the beginning of the story, are fading with the dying light of this long prison day. By day's end, the prison has finally taken a hold over Miller mentally and emotionally, and he, too, has become prison property.

The Real Deal
A Review of *Miller's Revenge*

By Charles Huckelbury

Only rarely does a reader encounter an author with the imagination and technical skills to animate his subject vividly enough to evoke a physical response in the reader. This is especially true when the author has no personal experience with the events he or she is describing. Robert Johnson is such an author, and his latest work of fiction, *Miller's Revenge,* is precisely that kind of evocative tale.

We meet Robert Miller, the novel's first-person narrator, immediately after Daunte McFadden has killed Jamal Jordan in a maximum-security prison in Baltimore. Miller is the cop assigned to the prison and responsible for investigating all homicides and ancillary other offenses. This is no whodunit; we know immediately who did it and where. The challenge Robert Johnson presents is to understand the why part of the equation.

Miller, quite naturally, brings a cynic's eye to his thankless job, necessary to inoculate him against the horrors that haunt the prison. But that cynicism doesn't disable his human response to the misery he sees daily. Early in the book he tells us, "It's a grim business, this dying in prison." This understated eloquence is of a piece with Miller's unconcealed sorrow for the human destruction he encounters and compassion for its victims. And yet he remains the cop with a cop's attitude: "Some call it snitching. I call it. . . doing the right thing." Thus the line between con and cop remains intact, adding to the objectivity of what Miller tells us.

Using Daunte's killing of Jamal as the vehicle, Miller gives us a guided tour of how maximum-security prisons operate, acknowledging pressures and circumstances that most readers will never comprehend. He discusses the mutually beneficial collusion between guards and cons, technically proscribed by prison rules but casually disregarded as an existential reality. His depiction of the modern prison as an incarnation of the plantation will produce nods of agreement by anyone who has ever walked the yard or been inside a cell, and his criticism of the drug war's disastrous human costs acknowledges the role that battle has had in making prisons even more dangerous.

Miller's narrative is not, however, unremittingly bleak. Johnson also gives us Vittoria Simone, the medical examiner who plays off Miller's cynicism in order to remind us that the dead men she encounters were once loved and valued as human beings, no matter what kind of self-inflicted destruction brought them to prison. In a skillful counterstroke, Miller tells her that he believes instead that some men in prison had "never been loved ...even as children."

As accurate as the topical and relevant ethnography is, what impresses most about this book is Johnson's incredible grasp of detail, from the appearance and smell of a burned-out cell to the technique used by Duante to kill Jamal. Most prisoners, including this reviewer, have a tendency to disregard prison-based fiction as irretrievably flawed if not written by one of us. Gaping holes in both philosophy and detail frequently emerge, simply from a lack of experience or insight.

Not so in Robert Johnson's version. If I didn't know better, I would automatically assume that Johnson had been there, done that, and gotten the tee shirt to prove it. Indeed, his description of the murder inside the prison's gym is eerily similar to a murder I, along with 240 other men, witnessed over thirty years ago, including the weapons and tactics of the combatants. Johnson even puts the correct jargon in his characters' mouths and reminds us that the prisoners don't "really live here like human beings," a position validated by the brutality of the murder itself. More to the point, the novel's denouement validates the title and prison maxim that what goes around comes around.

Robert Johnson is a masterful stylist with an anthropologist's grasp of his subject, engaging the reader as a participant-observer inside the unforgiving and refracted world of maximum security. Nowhere else have I encountered such a remarkable ability to describe the hopeless failure than massive incarceration has become, combined with an experienced, albeit jaundiced, view of human depravity and low expectations in an environment where life is lived according to the lowest common denominator. This book is a significant contribution to the discussion of social policy and the elephant sitting in the living room of every state's budget crisis. The genre is fiction, but the story it tells is terrifyingly real.

Miller's Revenge
By Robert Johnson

A review and commentary
By Kerry Myers

The first significant impression this book makes to a reader is the use of soliloquies and dialogue that seem equally competent for a screenplay as it does for a novel. It was easy to imagine the main character as an actor, spotlit in an archaic, dark and dank stone edifice called prison, thinking out loud about the nature of his job. The reader is present to his thoughts on prison and the people who inhabit it, and the system that builds and fills places packed with people sentenced to serve more time than God ever intended, people manufacturing lives and futures out of nothing.

The nature of the main character's first soliloquy, one that questions the very efficacy of public policy that makes little distinction and discourages discretion between those caught in the vortex of fear mongering and expediency, is all the more cinematic or theatric because the thinker is part of the system, a public safety investigator assigned to investigate crimes in the very stereotypical, multi-tiered, cell house-style, 19th or early 20th century state prison.

Interesting dialogue with a moderately young, female Italian medical examiner, someone without the unique American sense of crime and punishment, and who thus is just naive enough to ask relevant questions, feel the collective societal loss that warehousing prisoners creates, and show compassion for the humanity of each "victim" that finds himself on her cold, sterile table in the morgue, establishes the writer's uncertainty and even disdain for what the system has become even in his time within it.

Robert Johnson, through his alter ego Rob Miller, questions and examines the effects that hopelessness, despair and the innate survival instinct have on men confined in harsh conditions, stripped of dignity and subjected to daily assaults on their humanity. What, he wonders, is the damage to the human psyche? He senses the prison itself as the "beast" that steals lives, steals souls, steals whatever it can from whoever it can, even those whose job it is to "guard" the inmates by ensuring that the perimeter is secure and that clearing the regular counts protect the public safety.

Johnson describes a prison much different than the Louisiana State Penitentiary at Angola, where 80 percent of its prisoners live in dormitories and have regular jobs and are involved in a plethora of organized, sanctioned activities that occupy their time and their minds. But like the walled fortress he describes, which still exists in many places in the country, Angola is still a "beast" confining 5,200 prisoners, 76 percent of whom are serving life without parole and 62 percent who are now over 40 years old. They live, work and play each day in a large "bowl," the sides of which most will never successfully scale to see over the rim to the free world outside.

Through Rob Miller, Johnson creates a palpable portrait of the "beast" and the society that lives within. Trading and bartering, with commissary items and with people too mentally weak to stave off the assault of fear, is the commerce that oils the engine of this society. In many ways life in this prison, and all prisons, is evolutionary, the natural selection of leaders, workers, soldiers and those that become property. It is reminiscent of *Animal Farm* and the societal structure that evolves through natural order. Fear, violence, paranoia and a mob mentality are as integral to the *Animal Farm* paradigm as they are to prison life.

Johnson presents Daunte McFadden as a flawed, but totally human character with the same hopes, dreams and needs as anyone. Unlike most people, and like most prisoners, Daunte's life was dysfunctional, his wants and needs disordered, thus his choices led him to prison. But his humanity is not completely gone. He wants to survive, he understands the "beast" and how it preys on the weak. He knows the code of the life he lives and, to his demise, he trusted someone, a basic human trait that tells us we have value to another person. Rob Miller understands that the paranoia and fear perpetuated in prison, and specifically to the circumstances of

Daunte. Manipulated by information from another prisoner that there is a "hit" out on him, the perceptive truth of Daunte's world is that he is backed into a corner and left little choice about what needs to be done in order to survive. Daunte simply wanted to live, and so he took the only course of action known to him. Rob Miller did not condone but did understand the deeply running rivers that were at work.

The book is an indictment of sort of the way the nation deals with its prisoners, even those convicted of violent crimes. The subliminal programming term "violent criminal" often used by politicians, law enforcement and the media is completely misleading. Many people in prison are convicted of violent crimes but are not career violent criminals or perpetually violent. In fact, most people convicted of a violent crime are not career violent criminals. With the exception of the pathological personality, the truly mentally ill, and the career violent criminal, most people convicted of a violent crime made poor, life-changing choices in a difficult or stressful situation.

Johnson suggests that the policy of warehousing people, human beings, in hollow places of despair and hopelessness actually perpetuates the darkest part of society, one it would rather see in the reflection of a mirror than entwined in their real life. "It occurred to me, not for the first time, that human animals just don't live well in captivity," Rob Miller thought to himself. The punishment society metes out and the effectiveness of that punishment can be glimpsed in that statement. When is punishment no longer punishment but revenge? When does the effect of the punishment wane and the punished become either a cowered animal or an overly aggressive predator? When does the benefit for the public safety end if risk is no longer a factor, and the use of resources to continue useless punishment becomes immoral?

Miller sarcastically examines a commonly held misconception, born of societal ignorance of prisoners and public policy, when he speaks about homosexuality in prison, saying, "… it was better to let the men go at each other - and especially at the wayward teens sprinkled in courtesy of the drug war, some doing life without - than to subject prisoners to the horrors of pornography." Most prisons banned "shot books," slang for pornography, a decade ago in response to a growing public fear of sex offenders, thinking that *Playboy*, *Hustler* and other prurient magazines would exacerbate the problem and create a hostile work environment for the growing cadre of female correctional officers. In fact, the banning of these magazines has had an opposite effect. In Tennessee, the incidences of inmate sex offenses actually went up in the year after the "shot book" ban went into effect.

Societal attitudes are again subjected to critical commentary when Miller thinks to himself that, "at least with zoos, people bring their families to visit and have to be told not to feed the captives. Most of us would just as soon see the convicts starve, and we sure as hell wouldn't bring our families to see the carnage."

Robert Johnson does not advocate that prisons are unneeded or unnecessary. Rather, he indicts the system and the policies that perpetuate it by preferring to put people, humans, away forever in cages, out of sight, out of mind, buried somewhere where the rest of society does not have to deal with the real problems or the real ugliness. "I don't like to think of myself as a vengeful man," Miller says to himself after ensuring that Daunte's killer is put into the worst conditions in the prison designed to break his will and his mind, "but at times the hopelessness all around me in prison makes me burn with resentment, makes me want to lash out." If this can happen to a person in law enforcement, someone working inside the system, consider what Johnson is saying about those confined inside? What hopelessness does society continue to heap upon prisoners serving life sentences, many of whom are first offenders? What resentment does the system create when those trapped inside feel helpless to find redemption? It's a question "Miller's Revenge" asks but does not resolve—very deliberately.

Ariadne

By Hannah Herbert

In the corner of this cell, I'm weaving a web. Made of the finest gossamer lace, it's fragile, yet remarkably strong. It's perfect for catching moths and flies, but it's sticky enough to capture other things too: thoughts, dreams, secrets. So small and so well-made! No one would ever think to look here. When Joseph gives me his stories, I wind them up with my silky rope until they become so entangled in this labyrinth that only the maker knows how to find them.

I first arrived to this small room on the back of coat, a brown, unassuming coat that stood near the signpost I was dangling from. I had hoped the coat would take me out of the first winter's winds to some warm home where I could bide my time until the return of spring, but the coat had broken a law. He was set upon by three angry green uniforms and forced to the jail. He was trapped behind layers of metal and concrete, long bars and thick doors, loud clangs and sharp clicks—and with me right behind. The coat and I were pressed between the uniforms, like two foolish flies caught in the squeeze of a carnivorous plant. They pushed us down a dimly lit, grey passageway and through a squat opening that led to another series of passages, some winding and others angular; they made up a great maze with this little room concealed deep within.

The coat and I were thrown into this cell with such power that I was forced from my perch down to the slick concrete floor. The coat was hurt. The area where his head met the ground was colored red with his wet blood. One of his brown sleeves was stained too. He groaned faintly—like a panther downed by a hunter in the forest—but he did not move except for the experimental grasp of a hand. Was he dying? Was he breathing his last breaths? Spilling the very final drop of that liquid that sustained his body? I didn't know. And there was no human there to help him, to bring him to other humans who would know how to comfort his anguished limbs.

When I heard the drum of feet, I raced to the back corner of the cell, pressing against the dark blocks in an attempt to blend into the wall, like a raindrop against muddy earth. I became invisible, camouflaged by fear and panic. The bloody coat was heaved up from the ground by two new uniforms and pulled from the room with much struggle. I was enraptured to see the smallest signs of life stir in the coat as these uniforms assailed him, but he was still weak in his arms and legs and the others struggled with his heavy body. It seemed as if his torso, his limbs, and the rest of his form wanted to stay there on the concrete floor, but the uniforms made quick work of removing him, as if they had had a good deal of practice with this arduous task.

And then I was alone in this dark place, without even the nameless coat as my companion. I became aware that I was very cold. The walls were good for cutting out the sharp wind, but the blocks that make up the walls seemed to absorb the cool air, embracing it and taking it in, so that my corner was never quite comfortable. Those first nights it felt hostile. As if the very floor and ceiling knew I didn't belong there, they tried to force me out, with darkness and loud clangs and the sounds of humans who realized that they had been caught, like moths in a spider's web.

I thought that it must have taken quite some time to build a web like this, a web big and strong enough to catch and hold human beings. The walls weren't intricate and fine like those that made up my web, but they were hard and cold and rigid—the building blocks of a maze without exit. The humans housed here were now flying winged creatures, captured and petrified within the confines of this industrial labyrinth, only to be devoured later at the convenience of their captors.

I felt some sadness for the dragonflies and honeybees that had inadvertently landed in my careful latticework only to discover their own doom, but I think that even they must have understood that their fate was a part of a larger dance of life and eternity. I comforted myself with the knowledge that they were reluctant, yet honest participants in a world that, even at its most pure, required a certain amount of sacrifice. I imagined that these sorry flies and grasshoppers looked around at the whispering trees and the sullen rocks and the silly river and thought that it was fitting that their existence should end with a heightened awareness of beauty and hope. I was sure that they all forgave me there, hoping only for a small revenge: that I would one day expire in much the same way. Not one would have wished me here.

Where I come from the nights smell like new earth, dark and enveloping. Here the nights are opaque, impenetrable. There is no life to witness, no secret sunset world that only begins once humans are asleep. Fear pools around the edges of sinks and the bases of metal bars. I imagined that I could see a murky orb that pretended to be the moon, shrouded by clouds and abandoned by the stars.

So I waited. I built a web to hide in, to survive in, and I waited for something to happen. Some clue that would produce the key for solving this labyrinth.

I waited for twenty starless nights, until, on the dawn of the twenty-first morning, they brought Joseph to my cell. Three uniforms, but no coat. Just an orange t-shirt with a strong step and tense hands. The others gave him a rough shove into the cell, but he landed squarely on his feet, taking only a moment to straighten his back and gain his composure. I didn't know then that the orange t-shirt was Joseph. He was just a scared human, starring at the walls of the cell as if they could give him an answer, a reason for his being here and a way out. I could have told him that the walls were less than forthcoming about the secrets of this place, rather poor candidates for conspirators, but we didn't meet those beginning days of his imprisonment. His whole first day was spent in pacing, in sitting, in moving every which way, as if his body should be as active as his frenzied thoughts. He tried to talk to any human who would listen: guards, other trapped figures, an old, wrinkly human scrubbing the stairs. He was being unlawfully held. He had done nothing wrong. He had the right to speak. He had the right to write. But no other humans wanted to listen. To the guards he was an enemy. To the other prisoners and the man with the scrub bucket he was one voice in a chorus of despair.

When darkness began its rapid attack on the prison, he fell quiet. He laid on the pallet on the floor to rest his eyes and his weary bones, but he soon sat upright in the black cell. At first I though he must be searching, ready to make another appeal, this time to the night guard who might be more merciful, but soon it was clear that he had raised his head to listen. The painful sounds of the night had become a redundant chorus for me already, but for Joseph they were new and terrifying. Slowly, so slowly, he moved backwards, crushing his body into the cell corner that lay opposite of mine. He placed the side of his cheek against the wall and allowed the cold stone to mesh with human skin. Only then did his wide eyes close for a moment of sleep.

Over the course of the next week, he repeated his ritual, his outward pleas by day and retreat by night, with no answer or peace. On the eighth night, he finally cast off his small measure of composure. He released it in a howl around the cell, in a crashing jump against the walls and a pounding of fists. He was angry and vengeful and afraid and he threw himself against the far corner of the cell. And that is when I finally met Joseph.

The final thud of his body on the floor seemed to provide him with a measure of calm. He closed his eyes and breathed deeply, sucking in air through his nostrils and pushing it back out with even greater force. At long last he opened his eyes and realized that he had been sharing this cell all along.

He introduced himself with a good-natured laugh: "Hi, I'm Joseph. And who are you, Little One?"

Glad to see that this human was interested in civilized conversation, rather than attack, I responded in kind. I told him that I was a master builder, a spinner of webs so beautiful that even the hard-working ant was jealous of my creation. I had heard what he had said and I was here by mistake too, my only crime being that I was in the wrong place at the wrong time. I had never broken any human laws or really bothered with human life in general. Although I was indebted to several humans for their gracious hospitality in the colder months, I lived only for the unburdened air of my home at sunrise and the quiet existence that I shared with my graceful neighbors in the secret places unknown to humankind. I knew that this was something he could understand.

His face contracted with anxiety but his body remained as still as smooth stone. In almost a whisper, he replied: "I don't know how you've survived in here, Little   One. It's stifling. Eight days and already I feel as if I'm losing it. Do you think I'm going crazy? No, I'm not crazy. It's just that I'm frustrated and they deny me and I'm worried for what will come next. They'll think I know something, so they'll try to get it out of me or maybe they'll just skip the formalities and punish me for the things they say I've done. Maybe this is the torture, making me wait. Sometimes I think it will be all right, but then I remember my wife's face the moment they took me away. I love this country and its people with more honesty and passion than most men. How is it that I'm here?"

In truth, it was only desperation and chance that had brought about our meeting, but a shared love of freedom and the land would sustain our unlikely pairing. He shook his head slowly and leaned back against the wall, eyes directed at a sky that was not ours to see.

"I will leave this place eventually and I will return to my home. But I will not stop writing."

Bringing his gaze level with my corner, he added, "And, of course, I'll take you with me, my new little friend. There's a place for you, right here on my shoulder."

The hand that he had been using to indicate my spot swung down absently until it came to rest in his lap. His human eyes, now hard with confidence, were tucked away behind his eyelids. I watched my new friend as his limbs slowly unfurled and his chest began to move rhythmically in a slow rise and fall. I imagined that he dreamed of his wife.

In the morning, Joseph was alive with animation, on his feet and darting from one end of the cell to the other.

"It's all right you see," he said. "They have been delayed for one reason or another, maybe some missing papers or maybe they're too busy with real criminals, serious criminals. But they will come and question me and when they do they will understand that there has been a mistake. I am a respected writer, after all. They will recognize my name and know that I can have done nothing to injure my country. They will see that I am a patriot!"

He abruptly ended his speech and strode over to my corner, taking a seat on the hard ground. Balancing his chin in the palm of his hand, he asked, "Did I tell you I was a writer?"

In reality, he hadn't, but I remembered the things that he had screamed from the cell that first day. And, apart from that, he carried himself like a human who had imagination.

"Well, never mind," he continued. "I am a writer and rather a good one at that. So I suppose we are both builders in our own way, although we use different materials."

A smile still hugged the corner of his mouth as he began to tell the story of the beginning of his literary career:

"I was eight and I was walking to the school everyday, almost an hour's journey on foot. I hadn't learned yet how to care for school. I begged my father to stay home, to work, to do anything but study mathematics and history. But my father was a wise man. Even though he had very little schooling himself, he understood the power that existed in that school building and he wanted his son to take some of that power and claim it as his own.

"'Joseph,' he said, 'You are the laziest worker a father could ever ask for. How could I use you here? You'll go to the school one way or another, so if you can't be bothered to walk, then learn how to fly.'

"The following week the teacher told us about an essay contest. It was being offered to all of the students in grades three through six. The subject was: 'What my homeland means to me.' The prize was a brand new bicycle, shiny and red, with glittery silver lettering.

"Every night I worked on that essay, until the sky turned dark blue and the cool air rose from the earth. I concocted each sentence with precision and determination, laboring over several marked-up copies and battling with frustration. In time, I think I realized that I had won some sort of battle; I tamed the words with diligence and passion and I learned what I could say as a writer.

"When I brought the bicycle home, I laughed with my father. I rode it in circles around our home, taunting, 'How do you like my wings?'"

I listened intently as he built for me a picture of his childhood and his family. As he finished, he chuckled and shook his head: "Of course, I didn't pick up the pen again for another six years, but it was a start. And I rode that bicycle to school everyday."

His mood was jubilant with the memory of his youthful impertinence. Looking up at me again, he repeated, "They will come to question me soon. And when they do I will explain everything. You and me are leaving this place."

So that was Joseph's plan for escape: He would reason with his captors and lead them to understand that a grave injustice was being committed. When they realized this, they, as rational humans, would return him to his home and his wife. And when he had the key, when he knew the way out, he would take me with him. I began to dream of the stars again.

But the uniforms didn't come that day or the next, except to drop off food and empty Joseph's bucket of human waste. His euphoria remained, though, because he knew he had the key to freedom. In his good humor, he told me more about his life, about the little village he had grown up in not twenty miles from the city. He spoke with tenderness of his young wife Odette and his friends, all bright minds like himself. And then he began to tell stories; some were fantastic and unbelievable, while others were true to his own ordinary life. Whether it was a fairytale, a parable, or an honest recollection, he possessed a lyricism that would have been enviable to poets and journalists alike. He was a writer by trade, by profession and passion, and he created stories constantly. I became his audience.

On the fifth day after our meeting, the uniforms entered the cell. It was early, really still night, and I imagined that a faint crescent moon hung in the sky. Joseph lay sleeping on his pallet, arms and legs curled in towards his torso to protect himself from the cold and the empty space where Odette would have laid. He had only the chance to flick open his eyelids, before two uniforms grabbed him under the armpits and forced him to stand up. He opened his mouth to speak to the others, to ask if he could talk to the man in charge, if that was where they were taking him, but a blow aimed squarely at his stomach stifled his words. He gasped for breath, bending over and clutching his torso, as he was roughly guided out of the entrance of the cell and into the dark maze of the prison. His orange back disappeared around a jutting wall and I was alone in the cell, waiting to discover the outcome of his interview.

When he had gone I began to think about his shiny red bicycle, the one that he had claimed as a young writer. I had once nested in a similar contraption, although this one was banana yellow and it didn't belong to Joseph, but to a little girl human with short braids and two missing teeth. She discovered me there, building a masterpiece in the crevice between her tire and her little bike seat, and let out a scream that shook the foundations of my web. I only just had time to escape, but my creation was ruined and I was forced on the move. Now I could find the humor in such a moment, but at the time, I was deeply hurt. I thought that I had learned a lesson about the irrepressible cruelty of humans, even the youngest of their kind, but it was possible that I had made a mistake, that I had formed some skewed understanding to protect my own piece of mind, like a human who claims not to know the difference between a poisonous black widow and a daddy long legs. I wondered if Joseph would have cast me off if I had chosen to build my web on his red bicycle, or if he would have recognized a friend and comrade in arms even then.

As I wondered, I began to weave. I wove a picture of the bicycle as it glided along the breeze in circles around Joseph's home. I wove the large "o" shape of the little human's mouth as she wailed for her father's assistance. And I wove Joseph's plan for escape into my web with painstaking detail and attention. I wove the memories and the stories and the hopes and I waited for Joseph's return.

It was the middle of the night, long after darkness had fallen on the prison when he was lead back into the black cell, pushed roughly unto his pallet by an escort of just one uniform. His body was covered in sweat and little flecks of blood stained his t-shirt. Through the opaque night I could see that there was a large gash just above his eyebrow, open and angry and still wet with fresh blood. There was at least one large bruise on his forearm and from the way that he sat, leaning forward and slightly sideways, I imagined there were more on his back.

He was silent for a long while. I knew that he was alive and real only because I could hear his slow, shallow breathing as it crept across the expanse of the cell toward my corner. I was still too, waiting expectantly for an explanation, for some hopeful development. Did he have the key? Would we leave this cell?

Slowly and without warning, he turned to me: "Did I ever tell you the story of how I met my wife?"

He leaned forward, now with enthusiasm, his smile glittering in the darkness and his bloodied hands tense with excitement. Narrowing his eyes with mischief, he began, "So when I first came to the city, I was convinced that I was poised for greatness. I was one of the most successful students in the school and I thought that I couldn't be matched. A real arrogant son of a bitch, you know? ..."

Joseph finished his tale with a customary laugh, but when moisture welled up in his eyes, he let his gaze fall to the ground. He touched his fingers to the corners of his sockets, wiping the errant tears that had overrun his eyelids. Only a moment after, he raised his head, eyes dignified: "We need a new plan for escape."

The next morning Joseph was again taken for questioning, but he now understood how he should treat these uniforms, unwelcome invaders in our dank little cell. A writer, a human with imagination, is able to look at a life for what it is, but envision the ways in which it could be transformed into something all together different. He acquiesced without protest to their rough treatment, propelling his own body through the door without glancing backward in my direction.

While I waited for his return, I wove my ambitious web. I

was a master builder, but this was a stretch even for me: a web built with pictures, rather than geometric patterns. I labored tirelessly, stressing the bounds of my creativity and my craft. I wove a portrait of a proud woman with beautiful eyes who was Joseph's Odette. And I wove the sound of a human laugh, regal as the roar of a lion. I worked on my masterpiece, until Joseph was returned, just before twilight.

Both limbs were bruised at the point that connected hand and arm and red ribbons of color marked the back of the t-shirt that was no longer orange, but more of an angry brown, the color of scorched earth. But his fingertips were twitching with excitement. He took only a minute to catch his breath before he launched into conversation.

He had thought about methods of escape, about different keys to try. He was beginning to learn the maze. If they continued to take him out of the cell for questioning, he would start to memorize the passageways and turns. It wasn't as if he was completely defenseless. He had a few objects there in the cell, not very good weapons, mind you, but they could do in a sticky situation. And he had his wits. One of the guards would surely slip up and he would take his opportunity.

"I suppose there's no point in devising a window escape?" he joked, gesturing with ironic hands at the heavy, solid walls.

But the talk of escape seemed to have livened his spirits. After he wished me goodnight and placed his sore body down upon the pallet, resting on his stomach, I imagined that he dreamed of the key that would take him to his wife and back to his work. I hoped that he dreamed of my escape as well.

And they began to take Joseph almost every morning, leaving me alone in our cell to weave my web of stories while I waited. They returned him in the quiet of night with swift gestures and hard eyes. Sometimes he said nothing, but this was rare. He was born for storytelling. When he lacked the energy to lift his tired limbs into a sitting position, he let his stories fall sideways out of his vertical mouth, as he lay stretched along the floor.

Once he told me a magical story of a prince who was

transformed into a lion. The prince had fallen in love with a princess whose father owned a vast kingdom. A sorcerer, a rival for the princess's love, took the prince to a dense forest and turned him into a lion. The sorcerer told him that the only way to escape the forest and transform into a man again would be to find a golden antelope and slay it. When the prince finally found the golden antelope he realized that he had been tricked, for the beautiful beast was his very own princess transformed. Rather than kill his love, he took his own life. But the sorcerer's magic had undone him. The power of the prince's sacrifice broke the spell and the pair was married in human form.

That same night, he told me a similar fairytale about another evil sorcerer, but this sorcerer owned a democratic nation, not a kingdom. And he shared the nation with his comrades, other terrifying magicians. They corrupted the land and exploited the natural resources to solidify their power. The people became sick. They suffered and died. But the sorcerers continued to reign because there were so few brave enough to speak out.

On a particularly chilly night, he turned his head so that his mouth faced in the direction of my corner. He wanted to make sure I could hear his voice: "They came just before first light. They smashed the glass of the front windowpane and overturned a table in their headlong rush to grab me from my bed. They plucked me from the arms of my wife in my own home."

He pivoted his head duly, leaning his face against the unfriendly wall so that he could rest. That night, I imagined that he slept without dreaming.

In the monotonous days that followed, it became apparent that Joseph was losing hope. He wondered how long he could survive like this. He wondered how long it would take to find the way out of the labyrinth. I wondered if I would live here forever. If I would ever smell the fog again, if I would watch the raindrops as they crashed towards the earth or bask in the glow of the new moon. If I escaped, I would go to the secret world, the world apart from humans, and never leave it. I would miss Joseph, but if I stayed, I would miss freedom even more.

And then one special day, Joseph discovered my treasure, and also the key. His legs had been incapacitated by the day's interview, forcing his strength into his arms and shoulders. He pulled his head up and shimmied across the floor to my corner. After much exertion and angry language, he heaved his body into a sitting position against the wall and began to speak, but he stopped short, mouth hanging open as he starred at my creation.

"Little One, this is beautiful. How is it that you've never shown me before? And here I thought that I was the talent with my pretty words and stories. But you are genius," he reached out his right index finger and gestured to the stories in my web. With a smile, he said, "Here is my bicycle. And here is a little girl with braided hair."

"Ahhhh," he whispered, "Here is my Odette."

He admired the craftsmanship of my fine web for several minutes, remarking on my skill and precision with an expression of awe. And then, abruptly, he fell silent. He tensed his forehead and closed his eyes, as if all the thoughts spinning around in his head could escape out of his open pupils. Eyes still tightly closed, he began to mutter under his breath, "They never knew. They never even understood freedom." And he let out a sharp laugh, like the bark of a dog, before he relaxed his expression and turned his earnest brown eyes on me.

"Listen very carefully, Little One. I need you to do a favor for me. I need you keep building, to take all of my stories and put them in that masterful web. I need you to hide them there for me. Put my father and my mother and my little village. And put your home as well; put your friends and your green trees and your dewy mornings. Can you make a maze out of these memories so that they can never be found? Can you build such a web?"

I suppose that I had already begun the kind of web that Joseph spoke of, but I understood that he was asking for something much deeper from me, something that would require a lifetime's worth of knowledge and more energy that I contained in my own diminutive body. I would have to draw strength from the stories, from the memories and the love shared between two friends. I would create this web with the magic of the forest at dawn and the glow of the moon. And over time I would begin to understand that escape, like any other word, has many definitions.

I started out slowly, with the prince tale and the fairy stories, but in no time at all our very deepest secrets were given over to the web as well. I worked at the weaving day and night and Joseph worked at the talking. I carefully bound the brown coat to a silken thread next to the image of Odette. I placed the smell of the lazy summer breeze deep within maze and I wrapped it in the sound of the earth spinning on its axis. And I also wove this friendship that Joseph and I had created, this strange connection in such a dark place, so that it could endure beyond the cement walls and the metal bars, along passages made up of lions and raindrops and kings.

On a desperate night, after a harsh interview with the uniforms, a broken arm and purpled eye, Joseph pulled himself up on an elbow and struggled forward to sit. With short breaths he turned to me and said, "All the words. Don't forget the words. The sentences written by men who simply love to write. Keep them in our maze."

Two days later two uniforms, bitter and tired, came back to this small cell just after nightfall and ripped Joseph from his bed, arm still mangled. He had been returned from questioning only hours before and I wondered what could have caused this wild change in such an entrenched pattern. They forced him to stand upright and pushed him forward, through the opening out into their trap. Down a darkened pathway and around a corner, he disappeared from sight.

They failed to bring him back in the morning, but I trusted that another nightfall and another sunrise would find him safely enclosed in our small room. For I recognized now that we had the key, in a way that the uniforms could never understand. Sometimes I felt sorry for them. Raised by a city on the brink of chaos and nurtured with lies, I don't think they ever knew what it meant to live outside the maze, in a secret world older than time. They never even had a taste of freedom to defend. And perhaps this was worse. Even though Joseph and I have been left to live with the agony of frustrated hope, by virtue of our love of life and land we had already been given the key. It took Joseph's storyteller heart to recognize what had been there all along.

This was his plan: Together, we build a maze of our own. I would supply the materials and oversee the construction. He would offer the stories that were creativity and love and reality. And each word and each thought would be arranged so carefully in the labyrinth that no human would ever find them. They would be protected eternally and so would we, for we would place all of the best parts of our souls into that maze.

When construction is finished, we will be free. And Joseph will return to Odette and I will return to the moon and the stars and the sweet air of dawn. When they bring Joseph back with their stomping footsteps and their harsh touch, we will show them what we have created. We will leave this place together.

So I have begun waiting again, but now I weave as I wait. I weave the words and the feelings and the freedom and I know that they are forever protected. Never have I made a web with such grace or care, a web to match their intricate trap: just as precise, but much stronger, for their maze is made only of concrete blocks. This web is made of truth.

Ugly (Beautiful)

by Franziska Kabelitz

He knew it as soon as he spotted the uniforms. They had come for him, there was no doubt about it. They looked friendly, not at all mean like his friends had told him. Back home. They were doing their job, that was all. Only a job. They had done this a million times before. Routine.

There was nothing in the room but a row of desks with computers. One next to the other. A place of order, clean, cold order. Even the buzzing of the computers seemed to have some kind of order to it. He quickly glanced to his left, where Maria was hitting the keys, writing yet another one of these endless e-mails to her mother. Or friend. Or sister. About the movies she watched. About the restaurants she ate at. About the blue dress she bought on sale last week. Or simply about the weather.

An endless topic.

Beautiful, beautiful Maria. She agreed to marry him. Yesterday, swirling around in her blue dress, she had wrapped her arms around his neck, and he had carried her through the city, all the way down to that sleazy shithole they affectionately called their "apartment." Beautiful, lovely Maria. She hadn't noticed. He leaned back to get a better glimpse at them, balancing his chair on two legs. Risky. But then, what wasn't? He was used to risk. In fact, his whole life had turned out to be one big risk. And now his luck had finally turned against him.

Now they had found him.

Maria bought the "apartment" from a creepy online real estate agent, who disappeared without a trace as soon as the deal was closed. She paid for it with most of the savings from her hair salon job (which didn't pay well), and she invited him to live with her shortly after they started going out with each other. They had been living there for a month now. The movies were right: they always worked in teams, one big guy and his good-looking partner. Always a step ahead of their prize. He knew the play.

They had come to take him to prison. Or court. Or both. Or, even worse, they had come to take him back. He wasn't sure how these procedures worked, what the order was. Order. Prison-court-deportation? Court-prison-deportation? Maybe just deportation by itself. No long story, no big deal. America's prisons were overcrowded anyways. But he knew that at the end of all this he would find himself in front of his parents' house yet again in some forgotten village in Chiapas. Where the average age was more than three times his own. Because everybody had left. No jobs, no life.

Hasta la vista.

Maybe, if he was quick enough, he could just jump up and storm out the backdoor. It would take them a second or two to realize they had been on the right track. Enough time to make it outside. But then? What if there were more of them? What if others were hiding outside, waiting for him to make a mistake and storm through that damn door? He couldn't risk it. No more risk. Too much risk. Uncertainty. Hesitation.

It was too late, anyways.

Deportation. What an ugly word!

Punishment. But for what crime? Immigration. How can a human be illegal? Work. His work was illegal, even though all his employers told everybody who asked that George was the best gardener/ waiter/ Spanish tutor they had ever employed. Friendly, reliable, grateful. Always on time. Always with a smile on his face. He had told Maria that she was his soul mate. That he could not imagine a life without her. That he would do anything (!) if she agreed to marry him. To become his wife. His wife, who he would promise to love in good times and in bad, in sickness and in health.

That she was the most beautiful creature on the planet, seriously.

(This last line she had probably heard about one hundred times already.)

The shorter guy spotted him. They walked over. They asked for his ID. They were doing their job, that was all. Maria stopped typing and looked up, confused. Unable to resist her questioning ice blue eyes, he quickly bent down and began searching through his black duffel bag. The officer kicked the it, twice, and asked him to search faster. He found his wallet. Fake leather, stolen from a department store a long time ago. He handed his ID to the officer.

George Parker.

What a silly name. Maria picked it. She did everything. She cooked the meals, arranged a place for them to stay, cared for him. And she found somebody to produce this fake ID.

George Parker.

What a ridiculous name. Any officer would know right away that this had to be a counterfeit. How could they have been so stupid?

He didn't look like a George anyways. More like a Mauricio. Which was his real name.

At least, deportation meant home. Family, roots, identity.

Legality.

But still. Such an ugly word!

Maria had gotten up and was now standing pressed against the wall behind the officers. She was watching. The only other person in the room, a lanky receptionist who looked like the transition to high school had not served him well, remained at his desk, thinking that distance equaled safety. How wrong he was!

Beautiful, lovely, poor Maria. She did not deserve this. He had betrayed her. He had been careful, but not careful enough. And now she would have to pay for his mistakes. It wasn't fair. The life he promised her yesterday had evaporated into a heavy silence. Just like that, gone within a minute.
Killed by two officers.

Murdered by his past.

But that wasn't even the worst thing. The worst was yet to come. The worst thing would be his mother's eyes. These dark, deep, disappointed eyes. Sad eyes. Accusing eyes.

She had trusted him and he had failed. She had laid all her hopes, all her confidence on him. All of it. And he had promised to make it. But he had failed.

Large-scale.

He wondered if he would meet any old friends back home. He had no idea what happened to his travel buddies, the ones who crossed the border with him. Illegally. Maybe they were already back home, comforting his mother, telling her not to worry about her son in this distant country, in this strange country. Or, maybe they were still here. Somewhere. Living <u>the</u> dream.

What an ugly word.

He had used Maria. He loved her, but he had used her. In a perfect world, he would have put up that marriage proposal until they had been living together for at least a year or so. In a perfect world, he would have established a relationship based on trust and respect. Instead, he had taken advantage of her kindness, and he was sorry.

It's ok, it's gonna be ok, he wanted to tell her. *You will be fine, don't you worry about me. Forget me. Find a new boyfriend, one that marries you for true love, not legal immigration.*

But the words would not leave his lips. Fear had dried out his mouth entirely. Fear and the worry about what to tell his family. Failure. A whole ocean of ugly words. Maria, too, remained silent. Her eyes followed the scene, terrified. If only he could hug her one last time. If only he could look at her gorgeous smile, bury his nose in her golden hair that smelled of vanilla and honey. Feel the warmth of her body. Kiss her elegant neck. Tell her he loved her. Forever.

They handed him back the fake ID.

Come with us, the tall officer said. He got up. His arms reached for the duffel bag, but the second officer waved aside.

You won't need it.

He threw the bag over his shoulder anyway. Prison, deportation. No matter what, he could always use the bag.

Deportation. What an ugly word.

Illegal. Even worse.

As they walked past Maria, the short officer turned and nodded in her direction.

Thank you.

She did not move. Her face was white. Every color had left the usually so rosy cheeks. They had turned the color of an iceberg. Her beautiful eyes, suddenly hollow and dark, were fixed on the grey carpet floor. She would not look at him.

No problem, she whispered, her voice barely audible.

Outside, the dazzling sunlight burned on his face. The brightness forced him to close his eyes, drowning everything around him behind a dark reddish curtain.

He could not make sense of it. Beautiful, beautiful Maria.

Was it that easy?

Where would she go now?

CELL BUDDY

Story by Robert Johnson[1]

Adapted for the Stage by Ellen W. Kaplan, Smith College

(The stage is divided into two spaces: inside the cell, and outside the cell. The cell is small, a free-standing wall of bars defines it. In the cell are two bunks - steel cots, one on top of the other. There is also a chair and small table. Outside the cell is a corridor, defined only by lights, and a counter, with a shelf behind.

AMANDA stands at the counter. The COMMISSARY WORKER (an inmate) is behind the counter. On the shelf behind her is a Big Red Box. AMANDA darts glances over her shoulder suspiciously. Self-consciously, she clears her throat. Her voice catches, and she tries again)

AMANDA

Ahhh…one Cell Buddy please.

---

[1] Cell Buddy, written by Robert Johnson, was first published in *JMWW;* a slightly revised version was reprinted in *Lethal Rejection: Stories on Crime and Punishment* (Carolina Academic Press, 2009: 122-130).

COMMISSARY WORKER
(bored, barely looking up)
Which model?

AMANDA
Which…what? What do you mean, 'which model'?

COMMISSARY WORKER
C'mon, hon, people are waiting.

AMANDA
I don't know which…the standard goddam model!

COMMISSARY WORKER
Ok, Ok. Just doin' my job. Black or white?

AMANDA
Huh?

COMMISSARY WORKER
You want black or white? We're out of the mixed race buddies.

AMANDA
They make mixed race Cell Buddies?

COMMISSARY WORKER
We sell all races. This is equal opportunity stuff. Suh-ply and Dee-man - In de Can!

AMANDA
(embarrassed)
Aright.

COMMISSARY WORKER
Been a run on brown. So, which is it, black or…

AMANDA

White! For chrissakes, white!

COMMISSARY WORKER

Papers?

AMANDA

Papers?

COMMISSARY WORKER

They come with papers. Adoption papers. (AMANDA stares;
WORKER snaps her fingers) Fill in de Name, Pop it in de Frame.

AMANDA

What frame?

COMMISSARY WORKER

You're supposed to frame the papers. It's a respect thing. Sign
here.

> (SHE hands AMANDA the big red
> box. On the back of the box, we
> now see, it says "CB-WHITE" in
> bold letters. AMANDA signs for it
> and walks into her CELL

> AMANDA puts the box on the
> lower bed in her cell. She opens
> it, and we see the head and upper
> torso of the actress playing CELL
> BUDDY, now in its deflated
> position; the lower half of the
> actress's body will stay hidden
> within the bed. CELL BUDDY is
> inanimate, though at times s/he

> comes to life in AMANDA'S
> imagination. When moving or
> speaking, BUDDY is slow and
> mechanical.
> S/he is an object, not a person.
> Not *quite* a person.)

AMANDA
(opening box)

Let's kind of keep this to ourselves, a'ight? Not that I care what
they all think….but that commissary gal put me on edge. Whole
thing seems kinda sketchy….What's this here? A pump. How do
you like that? Two-part pump. Al-*right*, here goes.

> (As she pumps, BUDDY inflates
> into a full upper-body figure.)

Not bad. You can move some, huh? (At AMANDA'S touch,
BUDDY moves arms, swivels head) You know, some crazy
psychiatrist figured this out – what'd she say? Even convicts need
love…

BUDDY
(as Psychiatrist)

Prison is a lonely place.

AMANDA

No kidding. Especially if you're female. Hey, your arms move!

BUDDY
(as Psychiatrist)

The arms are expressly made long, to wrap around the prisoner's
body in a secure embrace.

> (BUDDY holds out his arms in an
> embrace. AMANDA backs away –
> she's not ready for this)

AMANDA
(looks nervously out cell door)
Warden thinks it's a big joke. Easy for her to laugh.

BUDDY
(as Psychiatrist)
Cell Buddies are smooth all over. (Demonstrates by holding up arms) No orifices. No - appendages.

AMANDA
We only craving sex, right?   Forget *love*. That's what they think!

BUDDY
(as Psychiatrist)
Your Cell Buddy will listen to you. Your Cell Buddy will make your cell a home.

AMANDA
(staring at BUDDY)
Yeah, well. Maybe. (To herself) Some of the worst things that happen to a woman in prison…happen in her cell.

                              (DAN, aka Danielle, comes into
                              the cell, slipping in from upstage,
                              not from the actual door of the
                              cell. This is DAN's ghost).

AMANDA
(to BUDDY)
You believe it? There's no men here, but we still got wife-beating.

DAN
(on top bunk, stretching out)
Amanda, babe. Didn't I always tell you. When I'm gone, you get yourself a nice Cell Buddy. Hey, Why be Lonely – Get Yourself a Rubber Homey?

> (AMANDA sits on lower bunk,
> next to BUDDY. DAN talks as if
> to himself. AMANDA doesn't
> want to hear DAN, but deep
> within, she hears every word.)

DAN

We were good for each other, weren't we, babe? I made you feel
safe. Dan the Man, your very own butch cell mate. Like having a big
tough older brother to protect you.

AMANDA

You made me feel secure. For a while.

DAN

Yeah, well. Safety's an illusion, babe. Specially in prison.

AMANDA

You were a smooth operator.

DAN

I was patient.

AMANDA

I was easy pickings. I was *prey*.

DAN

...for all the other tough butch cons. You couldn't have survived
without me.

AMANDA

I trusted you. You said...

DAN

It's either me, babe, or everybody else.

AMANDA

I shoulda seen it coming.

> (DAN gets down from the upper
> bunk, stretches out on Amanda's
> bunk. AMANDA moves BUDDY
> to the chair.

DAN

Hey, tidy up my bed, would ya?

AMANDA
(as she makes the upper bed)

But the whole process was slow, subtle.

DAN

Give me a back rub, would ya, babe? (SHE does) Oh, that feels
good, just like that.

AMANDA

At first you took it slow, subtle like. Ask for little things I would
have done anyway.

DAN

Warm up my coffee.

AMANDA

Then you gave orders. Like some perverted kind of King or
something, like in the Bible.

DAN
(tougher now)

I want my bed made, my laundry done, my food served hot while I
lay naked here in bed.

AMANDA

And sex of course.

DAN

On *my* terms.

AMANDA

On *your* terms. But mostly, you wanted me to be your slave.

DAN

You're a piece of meat, babe. (stands, grabs AMANDA, throws her against the bed) My punching bag. (he hits her, she goes down on the bed, screams) But only on my bad days.

AMANDA
(she sits up, rubs her head)
(to BUDDY) There are a lot of bad days in prison.

DAN

You *are* my slave. Don't forget it. (he lies back on the lower bunk).

AMANDA

And I didn't.

DAN

Rub my feet.

AMANDA
(she does)

I was meek, docile.

DAN

That's good. Helps me sleep.

AMANDA

Sure, Dan. Whatever you say.

> (DAN yawns, turns over on his
> stomach, sleeping deeply)

AMANDA
(pulls out a homemade knife)

He never saw it coming. (AMANDA plunges knife into DAN's back. DAN screams.   She covers his face with a pillow, then pulls out the knife. AMANDA speaks to BUDDY) I did it. I plunged it into his back while he slept. I made it, hid it, used it. This shiv saved my life.

DAN
(stands up, straightens his clothes)

It's a *shank*, Amanda. Not a shiv. Callin' it a shiv, that's gay. You put a *shank* into me. Killed me, you did. Now you're all alone.

> (DAN strolls out of cell and off.
> SOUND: prison at night. Low
> voices; muffled screams; stifled
> cries.)

AMANDA
(to BUDDY)

Prison at night is a scary place. You listen to the cries, and they tell you the thing you never want to hear, that the world is cold and hard and you are completely alone. (hugs BUDDY) Buddy. (AMANDA leads BUDDY to her bed, talks to him, touches him gently) Buddy. Stay with me, while I sleep....(she drifts off to sleep)

BUDDY
(softly speaks)

Could make stone speak of life's hard ends
With words that shine like darkling Gems
I was here
I am a woman

I bleed, therefore I am

AMANDA

Don't stop, Buddy.

BUDDY

Alive, in a manner of speaking
It's raw, sweet freedom I'm desperately seeking
A prison cell's a coffin reeking
Of dreams gone sour
Of life died by the hour
Of death by decree
Until you're set free
In this life or the next.[1]

          (AMANDA wakes, takes
          BUDDY'S hand, looks into his
          eyes)

AMANDA

Good morning, Buddy. (she gets up, starts to pump air out of
BUDDY – the actress 'collapses' again) I'm gonna let the air out of
you, cause today you're coming out on the block with me. Let 'em
laugh. Half of them have their own buddies. Just tuck you under
my arm. "You mess with Buddy, you come up bloody!"

          (AMANDA goes to commissary
          window. She has a shirt that is
          exactly the same as the one
          BUDDY is wearing. She carries
          the shirt carefully, tenderly, as if it
          were BUDDY himself. The 'real'

---

[1] Lines drawn from the poem, "Desperately Seeking Freedom," by Robert
Johnson. *A Zoo Near You*, BleakHouse Publishing, 2010:116.

> BUDDY is collapsed on
> AMANDA's bed.)

AMANDA
(muttering, to unseen inmates)
Yeah, I know what you're thinking. Boy toy. You got yours,
hidden in plain sight, what's that tucked into your shirt, puffing it
out like it's some kind of shank-proof vest. I don't give a shit.

COMMISSARY WORKER

No mail.

AMANDA

What d'ya mean, no mail?

COMMISSARY WORKER

Like I said, you got *no mail*.

AMANDA

Shit! (she storms away) Shit.   Haven't gotten a fucking letter in
ages…Hey, watch it! What the fuck are you doing?

> (SHE stumbles, as if someone has
> bumped into her. 'BUDDY' – the
> shirt – falls to the ground.
> AMANDA picks it up, furious)

You old bitch! What you falling on me like you can't stand on your
two goddamed feet! You got grease and shit all over him, the
floor's freaking filthy. Get out of my face, you fuckin old witch.

> (SHE runs back to her cell, where
> she pumps up the 'real' BUDDY.
> Still agitated. As she begins to
> calm down, she starts stroking
> BUDDY. Slowly, rhythmically,

> gently, she begins to make love to
> BUDDY. She lies BUDDY on his
> back, climbs on top, stares into his
> eyes, passion growing.)

AMANDA

Buddy…Buddy…

BUDDY
(sits up, sneers)
Can't you do anything right? I'm a friend. Just a friend. Clean me
up and let me get some rest.

AMANDA
(jumping up like she's been stung)
What the…Go fuck yourself!

BUDDY
You think I could really be excited by some lonely pathetic convict
like you?

AMANDA
(enraged, screaming)

Shut up! I hate you! (during this, AMANDA tears the cell apart,
bangs and throws everything, slams BUDDY against the wall, then
punches him the way DAN had punched her) You stupid plastic
faggot, you can go to hell for all I care!

> (BUDDY collapses on the floor.
> AMANDA stares, horrified)

AMANDA
(goes to him, tries to pick him up)
It'll never happen again, Bud, I swear. Trust me.

(DAN appears on the top bed)

DAN

It'll never happen again, Babe. Trust me.

AMANDA

(starts to cry)

I'll fix it. We'll start over. (she attempts to pump up BUDDY, as
at the beginning. BUDDY keeps collapsing over) We'll be friends.
Dear friends. We'll give it a go, Bud. We'll make it work.

DAN

(from above)

We'll make it work. (PAUSE) It worked for me.

AMANDA

(puts BUDDY on bed, snuggles up)

It'll be alright, Bud. We're in this together.

(BUDDY shudders. AMANDA
drifts off to a fitful sleep)

ABOUT THE EDITORS AND AUTHORS

Shirin Karimi (Editor-in-Chief) is an award-winning senior and honors student at American University, majoring in Literature and minoring in Biology while pursuing a career in medicine. She is the author *of Enclosures: Reflections from the Prison Cell and the Hospital Bed* (BleakHouse Publishing, 2011) as well as the Editor-In-Chief of Tacenda Literary Magazine, the Senior Co-Editor of Catalyst Science Magazine, and a Consulting Editor for BleakHouse Publishing. Her short story "The Desperation Diaries" was featured as the lead work in the current issue of BleakHouse Review and was recognized by the BleakHouse Publishing Tacenda Literary Magazine Short Story Award and her poetry was published in Tacenda's 2010 isue. Her literary works pertaining to educating the public on issues of criminal justice were recognized by the Victor Hassine Memorial Scholarship this past summer. Karimi has contributed her literary skill as a copy editor and proofreader for two published books, *Miller's Revenge* and *A Zoo Near You.*

Emma Lydon (Associate Editor) is a freshman in the Honors program at American University in Washington, DC. Her interest in political science originally led her to study the injustices in the criminal justice system. Emma hopes to one day go to law school and delve deeper into the fundamental issues in the United States prison complex.

Carla Mavaddat (Associate Editor) is an undergraduate, undeclared freshman at American University with a passion for photography and design. She is originally from Montreal, Canada, but grew up in Washington, DC. Carla is interested in human rights, and committed to giving a voice to prisoners.

Chris Miller (Associate Editor) is a senior at American University slated to graduate summa cum laude in May 2011. Upon graduation, he will be a JD candidate at Georgetown University

Law Center. Chris has extensive experience in legal research and appellate work, including paid legal research positions with the DC Public Defender Service and Boies, Schiller, and Flexner, LLP. He has also completed a volunteer stint with the Mid-Atlantic Innocence Project. Chris has recently co-authored a law review article arguing against life without parole sentences as applied to juveniles. This work is slated to be published in the University of Maryland Journal of Race, Religion, Gender and Class. In addition, he works as a Contributing Editor for BleakHouse Review and Tacenda Literary Magazine. In this capacity, he has published original poems, as well as selecting and introducing the poems contained within Robert Johnson's anthology, *A Zoo Near You*. For his work, Chris has received several awards, including the prestigious Victor Hassine Memorial Scholarship, two Outstanding Honors Student Awards, and a Trailblazer Award. Chris maintains a strong interest in prison reform and often uses writing as a means to advocate for those whose voices remain unheard.

Saba Tabriz (Associate Editor) is an honors Pre-Medical student at American University majoring in Psychology and Business Administration. Her interests span a number of disciplines, but Tabriz is particularly interested in the human anatomy as understood by science, as well as abstract notions of life, death, and everything in between.

Rebecca Weisenhoff (Associate Editor) is a Freshman in the Honors Program at American University. She is a Marketing major and a Graphic Design Minor. She is originally from Columbia, Maryland. Her first class in American University's Department of Justice, Law, and Society was Robert Johnson's honors colloquium Justice Stories: A Seminar, which led her to develop a deeper interest in the prison system and the injustice that many American prisoners face in present day. This passion has carried her through her second semester and has allowed her to write countless pieces reflecting on the prison system and to help work on the Tacenda Literary Magazine.

Robert Johnson (Consulting Editor) is a professor of justice, law, and society at American University, a widely published author of fiction and nonfiction dealing with crime and punishment, and the Editor of BleakHouse Publishing. His short story, "The Practice of Killing," won the Wild Violet Fiction Contest in 2003. His best known work of social science, *Death Work: A Study of the Modern Execution Process*, won the Outstanding Book Award of the Academy of Criminal Justice Sciences.

Liz Calka (Cover Design) is an award-winning photographer and designer recently graduated from American University. She is Art Director of BleakHouse Publishing. Calka has always been drawn to the arts and strongly believes in the power of visuals. She has designed many books and magazine covers for BleakHouse Publishing, and she also created the BleakHouse Publishing website.

Gretchen Cruz, originally born in Puerto Rico, graduated from The George Washington University with a degree in Psychology in 2009. She completed one semester at American University in the Justice, Law, and Society Department, and is now on her way to get a degree in Clinical Psychology. In the future, she hopes to become a clinical psychologist, with a concentration in forensic psychology.

Rachel C. Cupelo, originally from Upstate New York, is an alumnus of American University, where she majored in Justice and Public Policy studies. Currently, Rachel is a legal assistant with a small international law firm. She has been practicing her other passion, writing, for much of her life. She is the proud recipient of the 2008 *Tacenda* Magazine Literary Award for Best Poem, and the GLBTA Resource Center 2009 Academic Award. Her work can also be seen in *Lethal Rejection: Stories on Crime and Punishment,* and *BleakHouse Review* 2010. In the future, Rachel plans to attend law school.

Laury A. Egan's work has received nominations for a Pushcart Prize, Best of the Web, and Best of the Net. Two of her stories were selected for "story of the week" by *Short Story America*, where they were read in 56 countries and will be included in their 2010 anthology. Her fiction has appeared in *Tryst, The Battered Suitcase, In the Mist, Paradigm, Leaf Garden, The Maynard, Broomstick Books, Conte, Rose & Thorn Journal, Up the Staircase, Greensilk Journal, Punkin House Digest, Blue Moon Literary & Art Review*, and anthologies published by Static Movement Press and Rebel Books (UK). Her poetry collection, *Snow, Shadows, a Stranger,* was issued by FootHills Publishing in 2009, and a second volume, *Beneath the Lion's Paw*, is scheduled for 2011. In addition to writing prose and poetry, she is a fine arts photographer. Web site: www.lauryaegan.com

Zachary W. Faden, originally from outside Philadelphia, is an alumnus of the University of Edinburgh, graduating with an MSc in Intellectual History. He completed his undergraduate studies as a member of the Honors Program at American University, receiving a B.A in History and a B.A. in Philosophy. Currently, he lives in Northern Virginia and is a government contractor.

Tim Gallivan recently graduated with a B.A. in Political Science from American University. He graduated *summa cum laude* and with University Honors. Gallivan is now working at the Burton Blatt Institute, a Syracuse University-affiliated organization that aims to advance the civic, economic, and social participation of individuals with disabilities. He plans to attend law school in the fall of 2011, and he ultimately intends to pursue a career in public interest law.

Emily Heltzel is an Honors student in American University's School of Public Affairs, majoring in Justice with minors in Psychology and Spanish Language. Her primary academic interests include transnational organized crime, human trafficking, and juvenile justice. She is passionate about community service, and has served on the executive board of AU's chapter of Alpha Phi Omega, the community service fraternity, twice: first as Service Vice

President and then as President. Emily plans to finish her undergraduate degree in May 2012 and hopes to pursue her Master's degree in Criminology.

Hannah Herbert is a junior at American University studying History and the Arabic Language.

Charles Huckelbury has served thirty-six consecutive years in prison and is currently incarcerated at the New Hampshire State Prison in Concord, New Hampshire. He is on the editorial board of the *Journal of Prisoners on Prisons* and the winner of four PEN American awards for both fiction and nonfiction. He is the author of *Tales from the Purple Penguin, a* collection of poetry.

Ellen W. Kaplan is Chair of Theatre, Director of Jewish Studies, and Professor of Acting and Directing at Smith College, and a three-time Fulbright Scholar/Senior Scholar. She is an actor, director and playwright; she has taught and directed across the U.S., in Costa Rica (in Spanish), Israel, and most recently, in Shenyang, China; her plays have won awards and been presented internationally. She has published a book, *Images of Mental Illness in Text and Performance,* as well as poetry, prose and scholarly essays. Ellen is also active in theatre outreach; recent projects include theatre work with incarcerated mothers and adjudicated teens. Next year she will teach a course based on the Inside-Out Training Program for teaching in prisons.

Kerry Myers, 54, was born in New Orleans, Louisiana and grew up in suburban Jefferson Parish.   He holds a degree in communications and had a successful career in the private sector, spending eight years with an industrial firm in sales, marketing and producing training programs. He was convicted of second degree murder in 1990, though he has and continues to maintain his innocence. He joined *The Angolite* staff as a writer in 1996, and became editor in 2001 after the departure of longtime editor Wilbert Rideau. During his tenure as editor the magazine has gone through a redesign, won three APEX Awards for Excellence in Magazine and Journal Writing and a Thurgood Marshall Journalism Award. *The Angolite* magazine has a subscriber base of approximately 1,200 both domestically and internationally, reaching all 50 states and six foreign countries.

James O'Brien lives in the Phoenix metro area and grew up in Arizona. Writing struck him at a young age and over the years has encompassed just about every aspect of his life, aside from his day job. James works in the veterinary field, most recently as an anesthetic technician for the Humane Society. When he is not doing that, James writes, reads, and spends time with his fiancé and children (a Yellow lab named Boomer and a Bichon, Harvey, that when dirty closely resembles Ted Kaczynski). As subject matter for stories, as well as personal interest, he has spent years studying crime and criminals. James has taken a specific interest in the criminals when they are no longer capable of committing crime, as in when they are incarcerated, and how a person can be one way for so long and then, by virtue of isolation, become someone else, perhaps who they wanted to be originally. This duality of life is something James finds fascinating and he cannot wait to write more about such explorations into this facet of American society.

William Roth is currently a professor at Kutztown University of Pennsylvania. Two of his short stories have placed in national competitions-- Serpentinia and NMW. Three others have been published, one in Tacenda. One of his novels, "The Pelican the Pearl and the Live Oak Tree," a story about Charleston, S.C. during the Civil Rights Era, is due out in several months. William also has six books in print on academic subjects including ethics, development theory, and management theory. His most recent, "Comprehensive Healthcare for the U.S.: An Idealized Design," came out in January.

Sonia Tabriz is merit scholar and J.D. candidate at The George Washington University Law School and the Managing Editor of

BleakHouse Publishing. She graduated with honors and *summa cum laude* from American University with majors in both Law & Society and Psychology. Tabriz received the Outstanding Scholarship at the Undergraduate Level award from American University for her award-winning works of fiction, legal commentaries, artwork, presentations, university-wide accolades, and academic achievement. Having designed the text for *Origami Heart* and *A Zoo Near You*, Tabriz also serves as Text Designer for BleakHouse Publishing. "Empty Cell Windows," her first story, can be found *Lethal Rejection: Stories on Crime and Punishment*, edited by Robert Johnson and Sonia Tabriz (Carolina Academic Press, 2009:143-145).

Allison Whittenberg is a poet and novelist (LIFE IS FINE, SWEET THANG, HOLLYWOOD AND MAINE, TUTORED). She lives in Philidelphia.

TACENDA: n., pronounced ta'KEN'da – 'things better left unsaid'

www.ingramcontent.com/pod-product-compliance
Lightning Source LLC
Chambersburg PA
CBHW030208130726
47898CB00012B/934